We

BOOKS BY ALLY CARTER

UNiTEd We SpY

a l l y   c a r t e r

𝒟ISNEY • HYPERION BOOKS
NEW YORK

Printed in the United States of America

First Edition

1 3 5 7 9 10 8 6 4 2

G475-5664-5-13182

Text is set in 12-point Goudy

Library of Congress Cataloging-in-Publication Data
Carter, Ally.
United we spy/Ally Carter.—First edition.
pages cm.—(Gallagher Girls; [6])
Summary: "Cammie Morgan and her friends finally know why the terrorist organization
called the Circle of Cavan has been hunting her. Now the spy girls and Zach must
track down the Circle's elite members to stop them before they implement a master
plan that will change Cammie—and her country—forever"—Provided by publisher.
ISBN 978-1-4231-6599-6 (hardback)—ISBN 1-4231-6599-3 (hardback)
[1. Spies—Fiction. 2. Boarding schools—Fiction. 3. Schools—
Fiction. 4. Terrorism—Fiction.] I. Title.
PZ7.C24263Uni 2013
[Fic]—dc23   2013014093

Reinforced binding

Visit www.un-requiredreading.com

SUSTAINABLE FORESTRY INITIATIVE   Certified Sourcing
www.sfiprogram.org
SFI-00993

THIS LABEL APPLIES TO TEXT STOCK

For all the Gallagher Girls—

past, present, and future

Chapter One

The water was still as we walked beside it. A single rower sliced through the channel like an arrow shooting out to sea, and I couldn't help but stare after him, more than a little jealous.

"It's beautiful. Isn't it, Cammie?" I heard my mother ask. She slipped her arm around my waist. It felt sure. Safe.

But all I could do was muster a nod and add a not-very-enthusiastic "Yeah."

"Do you have an interest in rowing?" asked the man in the tweed cap and brown trench coat who was accompanying us. He looked like an ad for London Fog. Either that or a Sherlock Holmes impersonator. Or a bigwig British academic. And, of course, I knew that last one was right on.

"Cam, Dr. Holt asked you something." Mom nudged me.

"Oh. Yes. Sure. Rowing looks . . . fun."

"Do you row at your school now?"

He sounded interested. He *looked* interested. But I've been trained to hear what people don't say—to see the things that are better kept hidden—so I knew that Dr. Holt was simply trying his best to be nice.

"No. We do . . . other things," I told him, and reminded myself that it wasn't a lie. I didn't, however, feel the need to add that by *other things* I meant learning how to kill a man with uncooked spaghetti and disarm nuclear bombs with Tootsie Rolls. (Not that I'd done either of those things *yet*. But I still had one semester left at the Gallagher Academy.)

"Well"—he pushed his horn-rimmed glasses up on his nose—"Cambridge is a very well-rounded university. Whatever activities you enjoy, I'm sure we have them here."

Oh, I highly doubt it, I thought, just as my mom said, "Oh, I'm sure you do."

Dr. Holt turned up a path, and my mother and I followed. The long lawns were green, even in winter. But the sky overhead was gray, threatening rain. I shivered inside my down jacket. I wasn't as thin as I had been at the start of my senior year, but I was still a little underweight. Despite the fact that Grandma Morgan had spent the better part of Christmas break force-feeding me various things covered with gravy, my coat felt too big. My shoulders felt too small. And I remembered with a pang what had happened to me the previous summer—that even Gallagher Girls aren't always as strong as they need to be.

"Cammie?" Dr. Holt asked, pulling me back to the moment. "I said, what other schools are you—"

"Oxford, Yale, Cornell, and Stanford," I said, rattling off the universities that Liz had put on my hypothetical short list, answering the question I'd only half heard.

"Those are all excellent schools. I'm sure that if your test scores are any indication, you will have your pick."

He patted my back, and I tried to see what he was seeing. An average-looking, average-sounding American teenage girl. My hair was in a ponytail, and my shoes were scuffed. I had a zit coming in like gangbusters on my chin and a couple of scars at my hairline, which had forced a recent experiment with bangs that hadn't turned out so well.

There was absolutely no way for Dr. Holt to know what I'd done over my summer vacation; but there are some scars that even bangs can't cover, and they were still there. I could feel them. And I couldn't tell Dr. Holt the truth—that I was a perfectly normal senior at the world's foremost school for spies.

"And this, Cammie, is Crawley Hall. What do you think of it?"

I turned to study the big stone building. It was beautiful. Old. Regal. But I'd been living in an old, regal building since I was twelve, so I couldn't muster the enthusiasm Dr. Holt was probably hoping for.

"Our economics department is world renowned. Do I understand correctly that you are interested in economics?"

I shrugged. "Sure."

"Can we go in?" Mom asked. "Take a look around?"

"Oh, I'm sorry." Dr. Holt pushed his glasses up again. "The university is closed for our winter break. I'm afraid we're already making something of an exception."

My mother reached out and touched him gently on the arm. "And I am so grateful to you for working us in like this.

As you know, we're only in the UK for a couple of days, and Cammie has so been looking forward to it."

Dr. Holt looked at me. I tried and failed to mimic my mother's smile as Dr. Holt walked on.

"And here we have the library. Some might say it's the jewel in our campus crown," Holt added. "We have the finest collection of rare books in the world. First editions by Austen and Dickens—we even have a Gutenberg Bible."

He puffed out his chest, but all I could say was "That's nice."

"Now, up this path you will find—"

"Excuse me, Dr. Holt?" My mom cut him off. "Do you think it would be okay if Cammie looked around on her own? I know classes aren't in session, but maybe that would help her to get a feel for the place."

"Well, I . . ."

"Please?" my mother asked.

"Oh, of course. Of course." Dr. Holt looked at me. "What do you say, Cammie? Meet us back at the quad in an hour or so?"

Something seemed so strange about that moment. For months, there had always been someone by my side. My mother. My roommates. My (and I don't use this word lightly) boyfriend. Someone was always there, watching out for me. Or just *watching* me. It felt more than a little strange for my mother to nod her head and say, "It's okay, kiddo. Go on. I'll be here when you get back."

So I stepped away, reminding myself that when you're a spy, sometimes all you can do is go on. One foot in front of the other, wherever the narrow path might lead.

Before I turned the corner, I heard Dr. Holt say, "What a . . . charming girl."

My mother sighed. "She's had a hard year."

But Mom didn't try to explain. I mean, how do you tell someone, *Oh yes, my daughter used to be a real sweetheart, but that was before all the torture?* So she didn't say a thing, which was just as well. Dr. Holt didn't have the clearance to hear it anyway.

I walked by myself around the corner of the grand old building. There was an arbor covered with ivy. A statue of someone whose name I didn't know. The air was moist and cool around me. I felt alone as I walked between two buildings and found myself staring down at the river again. Another single rower slid across the water, looking backward, moving forward. It seemed to go against all logic, but the man kept pushing on against the current, and I wondered how he made it appear so easy.

"Fancy seeing you here."

The voice cut through my train of thought, but I didn't startle; I turned.

"So did you get it?" my best friend, Bex, asked. Her British accent was even thicker in her native land, and her smile was especially mischievous when she crossed her long arms. The wind blew her black hair away from her face. She looked alive and eager, so I held up the key card I had slipped out of Dr. Holt's pocket.

"Are you ready?" I asked.

She looped her arm through mine. "Cammie, my dear, I was born ready," she said, and then she walked up to Crawley Hall and swiped.

When the light flashed green she said, "Come on."

Chapter two

Crawley Hall seemed empty as Bex and I closed its doors behind us. Our footsteps echoed in the corridor. We passed heavy wooden arches and stained glass windows. It felt more like a museum than a school, and not for the first time in my life I walked down the hallowed halls of education totally breaking the rules.

"So, what do you think, Cam? Are you a Cambridge girl? Or do you fancy yourself as more Oxonian?"

"Oxonian?" I repeated.

"It's a word. Now, answer the question." Bex shrugged and leaned against a door that was unlike the others we had passed—not heavy wood, but steel. Security cameras were trained on it, and it took Bex a second to finagle her way inside.

"Cambridge is nice. It could use better locks, though," I said.

"So, no Cambridge." Bex nodded. "How about Yale? Or

you could always join me at MI6. The two of us together, out in the real world."

"Bex," I said, rolling my eyes. "We don't have time for this."

"What?" Bex asked. She put her hands on her hips and squinted at me. "It's winter break."

"I know."

"And we're seniors."

"I know," I said again.

"So aren't you . . . curious?"

"About what?"

"About life. Out there. *Life!*" she said again. "Tell me, Cameron Ann Morgan, what do you want to be when you grow up?"

We'd reached another door, and I stopped, looked up at the camera that monitored the entrance, and whispered, "Alive."

Thirty seconds later we were standing in the entrance hall of the largest library I had ever seen. Old oak tables filled the center of the room. Bookshelves thirty feet high stretched along every wall. First editions of Thackeray and Forster sat behind protective glass, and Bex and I walked alone through the empty room like a pair of extremely literate thieves.

We climbed the stairs and started through a maze of shelves and small alcoves perfect for studying.

"We should have brought Liz," I said, thinking about how our smallest, smartest, and . . . well . . . nerdiest roommate would have loved it there; but when Bex came to an abrupt stop, I remembered why Liz wasn't allowed on that particular type of field trip.

I peered around Bex's shoulder in time to see a shadow move across the floor. The lights were off and the corridor was still, yet a figure cut through the light that streamed through the stained glass windows, like a puppet in a show that only we were supposed to see.

I heard a door open and close, and slowly Bex and I eased out onto the landing and padded softly down a narrow hallway to where a door stood slightly ajar.

We paused for a moment, and Bex mouthed the words *You sure?*

But I didn't answer. I'd come too far—I wanted this too much. So I didn't hesitate. I just pushed open the door and walked into the room, my pulse quick and my hands steady, ready for whatever I might find.

"Stop!" the man cried. "Who are you? What are you doing here? I'm calling security." He spoke rapid-fire, barely breathing in between demands, certainly not giving us enough time to answer.

"Put your hands up. Up! Put them up," he shouted, even though he didn't hold a weapon. His hair was overgrown and gray. He wore a dirty, wrinkled suit and looked like he hadn't showered in days.

"Mr. Knight?" Bex asked. She inched closer. "Sir Walter Knight?"

"This area is restricted," he shouted again. "The campus is closed. You aren't supposed to be here."

"I'm not supposed to be a lot of things," I said. "My name is Cammie Morgan." As soon as I said the words, a shadow crossed his face. It was like he was staring at a ghost.

Me.

He was staring at me.

I wasn't supposed to be alive. But I was.

"You don't have any bodyguards, I see," Bex said, looking around the room. It was an office, not very big—just large enough for an old desk, a chair, and a short leather sofa that rested beneath the only window. There were a rumpled pillow and blanket, and the trash can overflowed with take-out containers and week-old newspapers.

"I guess that makes sense," Bex added. "You're not sure who you can trust, are you?"

"I know the feeling," I said. When I noticed that he was shaking, I added, "Don't worry. You don't have to be afraid of us."

"Oh, I don't know about that." Bex laughed. "He could be a *little* afraid."

Bex sidled closer, and Walter Knight backed away until he was pressed into his desk and couldn't move any more.

When Bex spoke again, her voice was so low it was almost a whisper. "Elias Crane the sixth is dead, Sir Walter. You probably heard about his car *accident*." Bex made little quote marks above her head, emphasizing the word. "Oh, I bet that drove you crazy, wondering if it really was an accident. I mean, it's possible he'd just had too much to drink when he drove his

10

BMW off that cliff. But when Charlene Dubois went missing while driving her kids to school . . ." Bex let the words draw out. She made a *tsk tsk tsk* sound. "*That* you couldn't chalk up to coincidence. So you went on the run." She threw her arms out wide in the small space. "And you came here."

"I don't know what you're talking about!" Sir Walter shouted, but Bex just shook her head.

"Yes, you do. Why else would you be sleeping on the couch in an office that's supposed to be abandoned, instead of at your London flat? Or your French villa? Or even your Swiss chalet? I have to say, this was a pretty smart decision. Squatting in a library. Clever. I bet a lot of people don't even know that Cambridge sees it as a feather in their cap for a former British prime minister to have an honorary office here. It's nice. It took us a while to track you down. But we *did* track you down, of course. And we won't be the only ones."

"The first rule of running, Sir Walter," I told him. "Never go anyplace familiar."

He was shaking his head and saying, "No. No. You have the wrong man."

"No, we don't," I told him. "You are Walter Knight, son of Avery Knight, great-great-great grandson of Thomas Avery McKnight. Tell me, did your great-grandfather change the family name because it made it easier for an Irish boy to rise to power in the British government at the turn of the century? Or was it because of the Circle?"

"What is your point?"

"I saw your great-great-great grandfather's name on a list

once." I put my hand in my pocket and felt the piece of paper that I kept there, while the image flashed through my mind. That list had been buried in my subconscious for years, but once I'd remembered it, I hadn't been able to forget it. The names written there were going to haunt me until the descendants of every last one of those men were collected and accounted for. "It was a list of very angry—very powerful—men. Now their descendants are very powerful people. And, as you know, Sir Walter, somebody wants you dead."

"Get out!" he snapped, and pointed toward the door. "Get out now. Before I—"

"Before you what?" Bex grabbed him by the collar.

"You won't be safe here," I said, and watched the words land, the realization sweeping him off his feet. He walked to the window and sank onto the couch, pushing aside the pillow and blanket.

"Does the CIA know you're here?" Sir Walter asked. "Don't tell me they're sending little girls to do their dirty work these days."

Sure, I should have felt insulted. After all, this man and the goons who worked for him had been trying to kill me for months. And failing. If anyone knew not to underestimate a Gallagher Girl, it should have been this guy. But in my professional opinion, guys almost always underestimate girls. And honestly, we Gallagher Girls wouldn't have it any other way.

His gaze shifted quickly from Bex to me. He looked between us as if expecting one of us to teleport out of there and come back with reinforcements.

"Your former . . . *associate* . . . Catherine Goode. She killed Crane. You know that, right?" I asked, but he said nothing. "And Charlene Dubois didn't just go for a drive and forget to come home."

"Charlene . . . is she dead?"

"Maybe. Probably. But you know Catherine better than we do, so tell me—why do *you* think she is picking off the leaders of the Circle of Cavan?"

"She's crazy," the man said with a scowl, and I knew from experience he was right. "She hates us. She wants to control things, and what she can't control she destroys."

I thought about Catherine Goode's son. She hadn't been able to control him. Did that mean she was bound to someday destroy him too?

"They're coming for you, Sir Walter." I shook my head. "And they won't be as nice as we are."

"I'm not in the Circle of Cavan," the man spat.

Bex shook her head slowly. "Wrong answer."

"I'm not!" This time, he shouted. "I'm not a part of that anymore."

"It's not the Boy Scouts," I told him. "They don't let you walk away."

"I'm finished. And . . . and . . . this is your fault." He pointed in my direction. "You should have had the decency to die when we needed you to."

"Sorry," I admitted. "I've been going through a bit of a rebellious streak. I swear it's almost over."

"So you're here to kidnap me?" he asked.

"You say *kidnap*. We say *hold in a secure facility until it's safe to turn you over to the proper authorities*," Bex replied with a grin. "But to each his own."

"If we found you, Sir Walter, then it's just a matter of time before Catherine does too," I told him. "Now, come on. Let us keep you safe."

I reached for his arm, but he jerked away.

"No place is safe. You don't understand. Look at you. How could you understand? You're children. If you knew what the others want to do . . . what the Inner Circle is planning . . . I never wanted this."

"Why?" Bex asked. "What are they planning?"

Knight shook his head. His lips actually quivered when he told us, "You don't want to know."

He'd seemed afraid when he first saw us, when he spoke about Catherine and the people she had killed. But in that moment, his fear turned to terror. He rocked back and forth, saying, "You can't stop it. No one can stop it. It's—"

"What are you talking about?" Bex shouted, gripping him by the shoulders, holding him still. "Tell us what you're talking about, and we'll stop it—whatever it is."

"You fools." He laughed. *"It's already begun."*

Bex looked at me. We'd come there with one simple mission: to find Thomas McKnight's descendant and take him into custody. We hadn't been counting on this. If the leaders of the Circle—the Inner Circle, as Knight had called them—were planning something, then that could very well change everything.

There was a new urgency in her voice when Bex said, "Look, we're asking nicely. When Catherine comes—she won't ask at all. So come with us now. Please."

The man snarled, "Or what?"

Irony is a funny thing. Maybe the room was bugged and someone heard the cocky, condescending tone of his voice. Or maybe it was just fate that made the sniper pick that moment to fire. But I guess we'll never know.

Suddenly, glass shattered, showering the room in glistening falling shards. Bex and I dove behind the desk just as the rifle fired again. I heard the hiss of the bullet, saw the dark spot that grew on Sir Walter's chest, and watched him fall hard onto his knees.

He was still upright, though, as I scrambled toward him.

"Sir Walter!" I yelled. He was one of the people who had sent a hit man on my trail, wished me and the list inside my head out of existence. But I didn't feel any peace. Whatever ghosts had followed me to that room, they wouldn't be satisfied just to watch him die.

"Sir Walter!" I yelled again. A drop of blood ran from his lips. As the life drained out of him, he toppled over onto the floor, never to defy us—or anyone—again.

"Cam!" I heard Bex call my name. She had a death grip on my arm and was dragging me to my feet. But I couldn't move. I was frozen, staring through the shattered window at the woman who stood atop the building across the lawn, picking up a grenade launcher and pointing it in our direction.

"Catherine," I said.

And then my boyfriend's mother took aim at our window again. And fired.

Glass crunched beneath my feet.

Blood ran into my eyes.

The grenade must have struck a gas line, because smoke swirled all around me and I could feel the heat of the explosion at my back. But Bex's hand was still in mine, and the two of us stayed low, crouching beneath the black air, running down the hall, away from the body and the flames.

When we reached the end of the hall, I looked out the window and saw Zach's mother running across the lawn. She must have sensed me there, because she stopped and turned, raised her hand and waved, almost like she'd been expecting me, hoping to see me.

And then she was running again, and I knew I had to find her, make her pay—that as long as she was out there, a part of me would never, ever heal.

"Cam!" Bex yelled as sirens started to sound.

Classes might not have been in session, but it was still one of the most prestigious places in all of England. There were smoke detectors and glass-break detectors, and someone was going to come looking for whoever had done this thing, and we needed to be far away when they did.

"Cam, come on!"

"She's here!" I yelled, trying to break free.

Bex held tightly to my hand—didn't let me go. "She's gone."

Chapter thREE

I've been to Bex's home before. She is my best friend, after all. But when your best friend is the daughter of two superspies, then that pretty much means your best friend moves. A lot. So walking inside the Baxter flat, I couldn't help myself. I looked around. New rooms. New walls. Same feeling.

Even though every spy I knew (which was a lot of spies) had spent the past few weeks telling me I was safe—that as soon as I remembered the names on the list, there was no reason for the Circle to try to silence me—it was still kind of weird to walk inside the Baxters' flat and have no one clear the rooms and pull the draperies tight over the windows. Instead, Bex's mother hugged me. Her father kissed my cheek. They asked my mom about Sir Walter Knight and told us everything everyone at MI6 was saying about the explosion at one of the most famous universities in the world.

But no one was worried about me. Or . . . well . . . no one was worried until I asked, "So what do we do next?"

"Now, girls," Mr. Baxter started, "I thought you knew that today was an exception."

"Knight is dead," Bex said. "Crane is dead. Dubois is missing. Along with her two kids," Bex added pointedly. "So I think Cam has a good point: *What do we do next?*"

"We go back to school," my mom said, taking over. "We go back and leave it to—"

"To who?" Bex asked.

"Rebecca!" her mother snapped.

"Sorry." Bex shrugged. "To *whom*," she corrected herself, even though I highly doubted that had been her mother's point.

"You didn't hear Knight." I shook my head. "He wasn't just spooked. And it wasn't just Catherine. Whatever the Inner Circle is planning, it's so big and awful that even *he* was terrified of it. And this coming from a man who has been a member of the Circle most of his life."

That was when I pulled the crumpled piece of paper from my pocket. It was in Liz's handwriting. Tiny pieces of paper clung to the left-hand side of the sheet from where she'd ripped it out of a spiral-bound notebook just a few weeks before. I'd folded it in quarters and put it in my pocket, and it had stayed there ever since, never leaving my side, always within reach.

The paper had grown soft and worn, and even though I knew every word by heart, I kept it. Part of me thought I might keep it forever. Part of me couldn't wait to watch it burn.

"Here," I said, slamming the paper down on the table where the adults could see. "Seven names. Seven," I practically shouted. In spite of everything, I still felt like I had to make them understand.

I looked down at Liz's feminine cursive, at the names I'd carried in my subconscious for years.

Elias Crane
Charles Dubois
Thomas McKnight
Philip Delauhunt
William Smith
Gideon Maxwell
Samuel P. Winters

"These men formed the Circle with Iosef Cavan in 1863," I told them.

"We know," my mother said, but I continued as though she hadn't spoken at all.

"These men survived him. And then their kids took up the family business. And then their grandkids. And so on. And so on. And now . . . Now Elias Crane the sixth is dead." I took a marker and drew a line through the name *Elias Crane* at the top of the list.

"Dubois's great-great-great-great granddaughter is *probably* dead," Bex added, and I drew another line.

"And now McKnight's heir is gone too." I finished with one more line.

"We've found three heirs, girls," Mr. Baxter told us. "Three is a good start."

I knew what Mr. Baxter was saying. The men and women

represented on that list weren't good people. They'd sold arms to extremists and assassinated world leaders—terror for profit was what Agent Townsend always called it. And I hated them. I hated them more than almost anyone on earth. But there was one person I despised more.

I thought about the woman on the rooftop. She had kidnapped me—tortured me—to get those names, and now she was killing them off one by one, eliminating the competition in the most hostile takeover possible. And I knew that if Catherine wanted the leaders of the Circle dead, then maybe we needed at least one of them to be taken alive.

"Three of them are dead," I said, drawing in a deep, slow breath. "But we still have four more names. Now we have to find the descendants of these men. We have to find them and stop them before they can do whatever it is they're planning next. Because, according to Knight, it is something bad and it is something *big*."

"That's not for you to worry about, girls," Mrs. Baxter said, and Bex threw her hands into the air.

"So who is going to worry about it? MI6? The CIA?"

We all looked at my mother, who put her hands on her hips. "You know that's not possible."

"Exactly!" Bex said, as if my mother had just proven her point. "The Circle has moles at every level of the CIA. MI6 too. And Interpol. Who knows where else? And *that* is why you need us," Bex finished, but her father was already shaking his head.

"This was a one-time deal, girls," Mr. Baxter told us. "Sir Walter Knight was a politician. An intellectual. A . . . nerd.

He didn't pose a physical threat, and for that reason and that reason alone you were allowed to come along today. That will not be the case for the others."

"But you can't do this on your own," Bex protested. "There's too much legwork. You need us."

Bex's mother folded her hands in front of her. "No. Actually, we don't."

I thought about the locked door of my mother's office, the parade of agents and assets who had been in and out of our school in the weeks before Christmas. The task of taking down the Circle was a mission so secret that only my mother and my teachers and their most trusted friends were invited to the party. Bex and I should have known that we wouldn't be allowed to stay.

"Where's Mr. Solomon?" I asked. "What about Zach? They've been tracking his mom, haven't they? Do they even know Catherine was here today? Have you talked to them? Are they okay?"

"Cammie," Mom said, "Joe Solomon is the last person in the world you need to worry about. And Zach is with him."

"What about Agent Townsend? Someone has to bring him into the loop. And Aunt Abby. She and Townsend are together, right?" I looked at Bex's parents. "Have you—"

"Cammie!" my mom said, louder this time, cutting me off. "That's enough. The two of you are already in this far deeper than you should be. And this is as deep as you go. For your own good."

Mrs. Baxter walked smoothly through the room and placed

her hand on her daughter's back. "Bex, why don't you and Cam go for a walk? Have some fun."

We both turned and looked out the window at the people on the street. I wasn't sure what was stranger—that three parents were asking their teen daughters to leave the house on New Year's Eve, or that Bex and I totally didn't want to go.

"They do a great light show at the Thames," Mr. Baxter said. "You can see it better from the park."

But Bex and I had both witnessed our fair share of explosions for that day. We didn't need to see any more.

"We know where we can find another heir," I said.

"Not now, Cammie." My mother's voice was a warning.

"We know that Samuel Winters's great-great-great-great grandson shares his name and is the US ambassador to Italy. He's probably at the embassy in Rome right now," I went on. "And Preston is with him."

"Girls, we are not going over this again. The ambassador is a hard target. He'll be safe in the embassy. And that means Preston will be safe."

"Charlene Dubois's kids weren't safe," I said, and thought about the first time I had met Preston Winters. He'd had an easy grin that had made him seem a little too eager. His arms were growing too quickly for the rest of him to catch up. He'd been a dork. He was my friend. And now there were people in the world who wanted to kill his father—maybe even Preston himself. People don't get to choose their families. Or their family businesses. Bex and I knew that better than anyone. And I couldn't help but feel grateful that at least my family business was working for the good guys. Preston wasn't that lucky.

"Are Zach and Mr. Solomon in Rome?" Bex asked this time, taking the lead. "Because someone needs to be in Rome. Someone needs to get Preston."

"If I know Joe Solomon," Mr. Baxter said, sounding sage and wise, "then I know that he is wherever he *needs* to be. Where that is, however, I'm not certain."

"But—" I started.

"But nothing," my mom said. "I'm sure Preston is fine, girls."

"She's out there!" I snapped. My voice cracked, and I hated myself for it, but I talked on. "Catherine is out there, and she's hunting the same people we're hunting, and—"

"And that is why you are going back to school!" I don't know if my mother even realized she was yelling, but the words were out and echoing around the small room. "You are going to go back to school, and you are going to have one semester where no one is shooting at you and chasing you and . . . We are going to have one semester when I don't spend every waking moment wondering whether or not my daughter is going to live to see graduation."

"We're seniors," I said. "I turn eighteen next month."

"Then act like it," Mom told me. The words hit me like a slap. As far as our parents were concerned, it was over. There was no argument Bex or I could make. We were beaten.

"Go watch the fireworks, girls." Bex's mom put her arm on my shoulders. "Go be young. Have fun. Enjoy the night."

Covert Operations Report

Operatives Baxter and Morgan were temporarily exiled from the London safe house at 2300 hours and told to go have fun. The Operatives, however, were currently unfamiliar with the protocol for "fun-having," so they decided to worry about their mission objectives instead.

The people on the street wore funny hats and sang songs I didn't know while they walked toward Trafalgar Square, Piccadilly Circus, parties, and pubs. But neither Bex nor I even smiled. She draped her arm through mine, and, as we walked, I was sure she probably looked chic and cool and European. I felt slow and clumsy and American.

"So," Bex said, "how did you enjoy your first collegiate experience?"

"Honestly," I said, "it didn't seem all that different from my high school experiences."

Bex sighed. "I know what you mean. If I ever reach the point in life where there are no more snipers, I might go crazy. Or bake. I could take up baking."

"Liz took up baking," I reminded her.

"Yeah, but I'd be better at it. I would totally rock baking."

But something told me she would vastly prefer the snipers.

The crowds were growing heavier. We passed middle-aged women in feather boas, college boys with their collars turned up. I felt like disappearing, there on that crowded street. And yet, I also felt like the most conspicuous girl in the world.

"It's okay, Cam," Bex said.

"What?" I asked.

"That's the fourth time you've checked our tail in the past ninety seconds."

"You're doing it too," I told her.

"Of course I am. Because I'm trained that way. Not because I'm afraid."

"I'm not afraid."

"After the year you've had, you're either afraid or you're crazy," Bex said, and I thought about Dr. Steve—wondered exactly how many games he'd played with my head—just as my best friend added, "And you're not crazy."

Bex gave me a smile that looked exactly like her mother's. Her words had sounded just like her father's. I'd never known anyone who was equal parts their mom and their dad. But maybe I was wrong. Maybe I was exactly fifty percent my father too. But my father was gone. Dead. And now I'd never know.

"Tell me again," I said.

"The Circle leaders—or the *Inner Circle*," Bex added with a wink, "wanted you dead so that you couldn't tell your boyfriend's psychotic mother . . . and my mother . . . and your mother . . . who founded the Circle back in the day. Without that list, no one would have ever known who the Inner Circle is. But you did remember, my brilliant friend. You remembered who was on that list, and now we *all* know who was on that list, and so the Inner Circle no longer needs you dead."

"Good," I said with a nod.

"I mean, they'd probably still kill you, you know? Out of spite. But there's not a price on your head anymore, Cam. You're safe now."

I nodded my head, thought about the other fear I couldn't shake. "Is Preston safe?"

"My parents think so. And my parents have a very annoying habit of being right," Bex said; but I just studied my best friend and maybe the most naturally gifted spy I'd ever known.

"What do *you* think?"

"I think Preston is probably safe for now. But he won't be forever."

"Yeah. And I just keep thinking . . ." I let the words trail off.

"About Knight?" Bex guessed. She took a heavy breath. "Me too. Fancy a guess at what he was talking about? If the leadership of the Circle is planning something so big and awful that even blokes like Knight are scared . . . then I'm terrified."

Bex is the bravest person I know. I'm not exaggerating when I say that. It is the honest truth. And I know *a lot* of seriously brave people. But right then Bex shivered a little—a whole body shake, like her spine was tingling. Like someone had just walked over her grave.

"I guess we'll find out eventually," I told her.

"Yeah," Bex said.

Neither of us said what we were thinking: that finding out was the part that scared us.

Then she turned to face me. "But we're going to win this thing, Cam. We are going to find the other descendants of the people on that list and take them down. And we're going to find and stop Zach's mom. We'll do it, and . . ." But my best friend trailed off. "One more thing."

"What?"

"Happy New Year."

Just then horns began to honk. Lights flickered. There was a blast, and purple hues streaked across the sky, shining down on the city of London. It had been a year since I'd seen Zach there, since Mr. Solomon had been on the run and my world had been turned upside down. I looked up at the fireworks that filled the sky. It was exactly the kind of moment when Zach liked to show up, say something cryptic, and kiss me.

I half-expected him to appear through the crowd, crawl out of the river in a wet suit, rappel out of a black helicopter.

But no kiss came.

"Happy New Year, Bex," I told my best friend, then turned and checked my tail, knowing there was no such thing as a fresh start, totally unsure whether or not this new year would be exactly like my last.

Chapter foUR

PROS AND CONS OF RETURNING TO
THE GALLAGHER ACADEMY AFTER
ALMOST A FULL MONTH AWAY:

PRO: Laundry. Sure, Grandma Morgan is an expert ironer, but the Gallagher Academy has this lavender-scented detergent that is maybe the most awesome-smelling stuff ever.

CON: There is nothing like being back at school to remind you that you have a lot of work to do. (And I do mean A LOT.)

PRO: Over the break, the maintenance department finally got around to installing the new judo mats.

CON: Bex, of course, had to challenge everyone to a round of judo.

PRO: Two words: Sublevel. Access.

CON: No matter how many hours we spent trying, we never could figure out exactly what the Circle was up to.

———

I know I shouldn't admit it, but I wasn't exactly looking forward to the rest of the students coming back to school. Bex and I had been alone with my mom and the other teachers for three whole days by then, and there was something nice about it. No lines in the Grand Hall, no crowds on the stairs. I could use all the hot water I wanted in the shower. But most of all, I totally wasn't looking forward to—

"What happened?"

Sure, they call me the Chameleon, but when it comes to getting lost in the crowds at the Gallagher Academy, Liz really is quite a natural. After all, that afternoon the halls were full of girls and teachers, piles of backpacks and suitcases lining the halls, and even though we're seniors and all, Liz was lost in a throng of freshmen and sophomores.

But as she grabbed me by the arm and pulled me into a quiet alcove, I couldn't help but remember that the start of a new semester meant questions—lots of questions. And the hardest ones weren't going to be coming from our teachers.

"So . . . what happened over break? Where did you go? Who did you see? What do the Baxters think about Preston, and . . . oh . . . Just tell me what happened!"

Technically, the answer was classified. We were in an unsecured alcove with far too many highly trained ears and eyes around. I could have given any of those excuses, but I didn't have to, because just then Bex stepped into the alcove and said, "She's here."

* * *

Now, to be technical about it, there were a whole lot of girls there, but I knew exactly who Bex meant. What I didn't know was why she was leading us down the main staircase and through the foyer that served as the official front door of our school.

Out front, at least a dozen limos and town cars were lining up to deliver our classmates, but Bex broke into a full run, darting around the corner of the building.

"Bex," Liz cried, "slow down. Where are we . . ."

But then Liz couldn't finish. She was too transfixed by the sight of the swirling blades of the helicopter that was slowly coming to rest on our school's back lawn.

"I'll hand it to Macey," Bex said. "She still knows how to make an entrance."

We were used to some pomp and circumstance, but even for Macey McHenry, a helicopter arrival seemed a little over the top. But then I realized that Macey wasn't alone.

My mother was walking around the corner of the mansion, waving to a man in a trench coat and scarf who was offering a hand to help Macey climb out of the helicopter.

"Senator," my mom said, shouting over the roar of the engines. "What a nice surprise."

She sounded like she'd been expecting him, but considering the fact that our school wasn't going on full automatic lockdown, my mother must have had it on good authority that he wasn't coming inside.

"Hello, Mrs. Morgan," Senator McHenry said, taking my mother's hand. Then he seemed to notice Bex, Liz, and me. "Girls," he added.

Macey was quiet beside her father. She looked thinner than I remembered. Her usually bright blue eyes were duller. Worried.

"Hello, Senator. It's so nice to see you again," Bex said in her best American accent, harkening back to the role she'd played so well the very first time Macey had ever set foot on our campus. "To what do we owe the pleasure?"

"Oh, just dropping Macey off," he said. "I'm sorry for the intrusion, but with all that has gone on in the past few weeks . . . It seems being a public figure has become a bit of a hazardous job. I mean, did you hear about that woman from the European Union? Dubois, I think her name was."

"I did," Mom said.

"And then Sir Walter Knight," the senator went on. "I can't believe it. If a man isn't safe at Cambridge . . ." The senator shook his head then looked into my mother's eyes. "I got acquainted with him during the campaign, you see. He and Ambassador Winters were close. Knight was a top advisor."

"Oh. I wasn't aware of that," Mom said, even though she was very well aware of it all. In fact, she knew more about what was going on than even the senior senator from Virginia, but that's part of the job, sometimes. Shaking your head. Saying the right things instead of the truth.

"I wanted to make sure Macey got here safely." He squeezed his daughter's shoulders, and Macey didn't pull away. In fact, she didn't do anything. I wondered if maybe that was what I'd looked like the semester before, climbing out of a helicopter, numb and too thin. But exactly why Macey looked that way I wasn't really sure.

"Now, Macey, you have a good semester." He patted her awkwardly on the arm.

"Yes, Father."

"Study hard and . . . enjoy yourself."

"Yes, Father."

"And . . . good-bye."

I waited for him to give her a hug, kiss her cheek. But Macey's father just hunched low and walked back to the chopper. Once inside, he gave us a textbook politician's wave, and then he was rising, disappearing into the sky over Virginia.

Three months before, when I had found my father's grave, I'd tried to claw through the frozen earth with just my bare hands—I'd been willing to do anything just be closer to him. As the cold air whirled around us, I thought back to the way I'd felt then, and I looked at Macey, who hadn't even watched as her own dad took flight.

"So, Macey," Liz started slowly, "how was your—"

"Where is he?" Macey asked, cutting Liz off and spinning, looking at my mother.

"Who?" Mom asked, but I already knew the answer.

"Preston. He's here, right?" There was a hopefulness about Macey, but a desperation too as she asked, "You did get him, didn't you?"

"Macey," my mother said, reaching for her, "you have to understand—"

"No," Macey snapped. "I don't have to do anything." Her father's helicopter looked like a wasp on the horizon.

"The US Embassy in Rome is one of the most secure buildings in Europe. Preston's father is a powerful man. He's safe," Mom said, then repeated, "Preston is *safe*."

"I heard Elias Crane the sixth had a car accident," Macey said. "And Charlene Dubois and her kids disappeared? Her kids!" Macey had a point, and she knew it. It wasn't just the leaders of the Circle who were getting hurt. Their kids were getting caught in the crossfire. Which meant Preston wasn't as safe as any of us wanted to believe.

"I wasn't living in a cave, you know," Macey told us. "These things make the news. And every day I waited for the news that the American Embassy in Rome had been attacked."

"That didn't happen, Macey," I told her.

"But it will." Macey was so certain, and the worst part was that she was right. "So when are you going to get him?"

"When the time is right, Macey. And only when the time is right." My mom sounded like a headmistress, a senior operative, someone who had lived most of her life on a need-to-know basis. And as far as she was concerned, we absolutely, positively did *not* need to know.

"But—" Liz started. She hadn't had spies as parents. Unlike Bex and me, she still didn't know the signs that a conversation was over.

"That is all, girls. You go settle in," Mom told Macey. "I'll see you all at the Welcome Back Dinner."

And then she turned. A cold wind blew across the grounds. Her dark hair spiraled around her, and she walked so tall, so straight. And I knew Rachel Morgan wasn't going to cave, not to the likes of us.

Macey must have known it too, because there was fire in her eyes when she said, "Tell me everything."

Bex and I shared a look, then Bex lowered her voice. "We'd better go inside."

The halls were starting to clear out as we made our way through the mansion. Loud music boomed out of a few rooms. There were showers running on almost every floor. It sounded like the start of a new semester, but when we reached the suite I shared with my three closest friends in the world, it hit me: this wasn't a regular semester. It was our *last* semester.

"Okay. We're inside. No eavesdropping freshmen here, so are you three going to tell me what's going on or aren't you?" Macey asked, spinning on us all and slamming the door. "Because I know Cam didn't get that scratch on her cheek from shaving."

Absentmindedly, I reached up and touched my face, the last remaining trace of Cambridge and Knight and our encounter with my boyfriend's mother. I know childhood is supposed to scar you, but mine seemed to be going to extremes.

"I got this in England. Cambridge," I said, clarifying.

"You were there?" Liz asked. "With Knight?"

"Yeah," I admitted. Something about the memory sent a

shiver down my spine. "We went to try to get him, bring him into custody, you know? But Zach's mom was there, and we weren't quite quick enough."

"Why him?" Macey asked. She was bristling against even us. "Why did *he* get to be saved?" she demanded.

"He wasn't saved! We were too late," I shouted. "We were there to take him into custody. And then he started rambling on and on about how he had left the Inner Circle because they were planning some big, huge, terrible thing. He said it had already started."

"What was it?" Liz asked, but Bex just shook her head.

"Before he could tell us . . . he died."

"No," I said, and I felt myself growing cold and angry. "Before he could tell us, Zach's mother murdered him."

Down the hall, music was blaring. Girls rushed past, looking for lost suitcases and misplaced uniform skirts; but in our suite, the real world was taking over. It was already long past graduation.

"So you didn't even try to save Preston?" Macey's blue eyes turned to ice.

"Preston Winters is not a soft target, Macey," Bex snapped. They weren't the comforting words of a friend. They were the analysis of an operative, and that was exactly what Macey needed then. "His father knows that Catherine is hunting down members of the Inner Circle, and he's no doubt taking precautions. He's also a US ambassador in a major post, which means embassy protection. Which means anti-terror roadblocks and biohazard detectors, bulletproof limousines and marines. *It means marines*, Macey. So Preston isn't out there on his own. He lives in a fortress with a whole lot of people whose job it is to step between him and a bullet, so pull yourself together. Preston is fine. And if he's not our mission at the moment, then he's not our mission. Do you get that?"

It took her a moment, but eventually Macey nodded. She walked to her closet and threw open the doors, pulled out a plaid skirt, and started getting undressed.

"What are you doing?" Bex asked.

Macey looked at her like she was an idiot. "Welcome Back Dinner," she said, not only as though the fight was over but like it had never happened at all.

"So you're . . ." I started slowly, carefully choosing my words, "okay?"

"Sure. Fine. Let's just go to dinner," Macey said, but none of us moved.

"Oh, you guys," Liz exclaimed after a moment, and then she started to cry.

"Liz, what's—" I started, but her wails cut me off.

"It's our last Welcome Back Dinner!"

Bex tried to comfort her. (But Bex is really better at inflicting pain than softening it.) I wanted to say something. But all I could do was remember that of all of Liz's many, many skills, pretty-crying definitely isn't one of them.

Bex looked at me, a silent thought coursing between us. It was going to be a very long semester.

Chapter five

Walking down the stairs that night, most of the senior class around me, I couldn't shake the feeling that it had been forever since I'd been to a Welcome Back Dinner. Then I stopped cold, one hand on the banister of the Grand Stairs, realizing it hadn't been forever. It had been a year. (And let's face it, a year is pretty much forever in teenage girl time.)

"What is it, Cam?" Bex asked. The rest of the group was walking on toward the doors like conquering heroes.

Like seniors.

But I was still frozen where I stood.

"Cam," Bex said again, "what's wrong?"

What was I supposed to say? That Liz was right, and the whole night was a little too symbolic-slash-scary? That Macey was right, and marine protection or not, Preston wasn't going to be safe until he was far away from his father? Or that Bex herself was right—that we were operatives, and we just had to keep our eyes on our mission?

So I didn't say anything.

"Don't freak," Bex said, almost like she'd read my mind.

"I'm not freaking," I said.

"Because you look like you're freaking."

I turned my gaze to her and let my guard down. "I haven't done one of these in a while," I said.

"I know. But I don't think that's the problem."

"It's not?"

"Nope." Bex shook her head and walked down a couple of stairs. "I think you're freaked about what happened at Cambridge. I think it scared you."

"I've been through worse, Bex," I said, joining her on the lower stairs. "Way worse."

"Oh, not the attack." Bex raised a finger in contradiction. "What happened *before* the attack. I think you saw the future. Which is kind of freaky when—two months ago—you didn't think you were going to have one."

"So . . . Cammie . . ." Tina Walters started as soon as I'd found my seat at the senior table. None of the teachers were inside yet, and the hall was filled with chattering and laughing, but something else, too. Tina leaned closer, her voice no louder than a conspiratorial whisper, "What have *you* heard?"

"About what, Tina?" I said. Honestly, I wasn't surprised. Tina wasn't just the Gallagher Academy's self-appointed director of communications (aka school big mouth). She was also the daughter of one of the school's leading alums, who happens to pose as D.C.'s most powerful gossip columnist. So conspiratorial whispers are kind of Tina's stock-in-trade.

"About that huge oil tanker that exploded in the Caspian Sea, of course!" she said as if natural and geopolitical disasters were common Gallagher Academy conversation. And . . . well . . . I guess they kind of were. "What do *you* think really happened?" Tina asked.

It had been in the news, of course. I'd heard about it. Everyone had heard about it. But even for spy girls, it was an unusual topic.

"Because *my* sources say it was no accident," Tina said before I'd had the chance to utter a word. "Every Iranian port on the Caspian has been shut down because of it. And trust me, if there is one thing the Iranians like, it's oil. If there are two things they like, it's oil and their ability to ship it to potential buyers."

"How about that bridge explosion in Azerbaijan?" Courtney Bauer asked.

Liz wheeled on her. "What about it?"

"Mom said there was a bomb on the train," Courtney said.

"A bomb?" Liz asked.

"Yeah." Courtney stirred the ice in her glass almost absentmindedly as she answered. "I'm pretty sure she was the one who separated that car from the rest of the train before it blew."

"She saved a lot of lives," Bex said, but Courtney tried to shrug it off.

"It wasn't a big deal," she said, even though it was. After all, it's hard to admit that your mom did something really scary without also admitting that, next time, she might not be so lucky.

"So . . ." Tina went on, "Cammie, what do you know about it?"

"Nothing," I said, but Tina just looked at me. "Really," I told her. "I don't know anything. I was in England with Bex's parents."

"Ooh, did you hear about that former prime minister who got blown up at Cambridge? It was supposedly an accident, but my sources say it wasn't. What do you know about that?" Tina tried again.

I could have lied to her. I *would* have lied to her. My school had taught me how. My circumstances took away almost all of the guilt. I was just about to do exactly that when the doors at the back of the room swung open and our teachers walked in. As their long procession moved down the center aisle, a new thought filled my mind.

"Where's Zach?" I scanned the room. "And Mr. Solomon? Where are they?" I asked.

Macey gave me an *It's not fun, is it?* look, but I didn't have time to consider the irony. Or the hypocrisy. Honestly, there's such a fine line between the two that sometimes it makes my head hurt.

I'd always assumed that Zach and Mr. Solomon would be back for the start of school and, technically, school began with the Welcome Back Dinner. But Zach and Mr. Solomon were nowhere to be seen.

Before anyone could answer, my mother took her place at the front of the room and said, "Women of the Gallagher Academy, who comes here?"

In unison, every girl in the room stood and said, "We are the sisters of Gillian."

With every line of our motto I felt a tug, not just in my heart but in my head. We were sisters. And that wasn't going to end with graduation. We would honor her sword and guard her secrets with our lives. Our school's motto made it sound so easy, so grand. There in that beautiful building with our perfectly pressed skirts, it was supposed to be so simple. Gallagher Girls = Good. But it wasn't. I knew it. I'd seen it. I'd heard Zach's mother brag about being a member of my sisterhood. Looking around the room, I couldn't help but wonder if there were any traitors in our midst even then.

"I hope you all had an excellent break," my mother said from the front of the room. "It's very good to see you back here, safe and sound." She took a breath, letting the words settle over us. Then she shuffled some papers on the podium, checking notes she probably didn't need.

"Now, eighth grade, your suites will be undergoing a complete bug sweep—that's insects, not listening devices. Please be prepared for some brief interruptions in the next week and use the back stairwell for the time being, as we have found termites in the front. Sophomores, Professor Buckingham tells me that many of you have yet to turn in your Track Declaration Forms. Those must be filled out before classes begin tomorrow morning. Trust me, ladies, this is not how you want to begin your careers. And, seniors . . . congratulations. I'm very proud of you, and I'm very excited for you to begin our career assessment program. The first event is in two weeks. Please see Madame Dabney for the complete schedule."

Mom looked down at her list one final time, then folded the paper. "I guess that's it. Welcome back, girls. And have a great semester."

She smiled out across the room. It was like a spotlight, so bright and hopeful and happy. When my mother looked like that, it was easy to believe that there was no evil in the world. I wanted to know if she was faking or forgetting. Whatever the case, I was hoping our last semester at spy school would teach us how to do that for ourselves.

That night, our suite was unusually quiet. It was the first night back, after all. We didn't have any tests or homework. There should have been movie marathons and makeovers. Liz should have been clamoring for extra credit; but even she was silent as we sat on our beds, none of us talking.

"What is it, Lizzie?" Bex tried to tease. "Have you reached your lifetime limit for bonus points?"

Usually a remark like that would make Liz go white and ask whether or not a limit to extra credit was an actual thing. Then she'd dig out her Gallagher Academy Student Handbook just to make sure. But she didn't do either. And that, let me tell you, was scary.

"Seriously." Bex moved to Liz's bed. "What is it?"

"Nothing." Liz stood and picked up a bundle of clothes, starting for the bathroom. "It's nothing."

"Liar." Bex cut her off.

On her bed, Macey shifted to study us. But she didn't mention Preston again. She didn't ask about Cambridge.

"It's nothing, Bex. I'm just tired." Again, Liz tried to go to the bathroom, but again, Bex cut her off.

"Try again."

Right then it was like all the nostalgia had been drained from Liz. She had a brand-new encryption textbook, but she wasn't giddy. There was a stack of *Microbiology Monthlys* waiting for her, but she hadn't even picked them up. Liz wasn't being Liz, and Bex was right not to like it.

"What is it, Liz?" I asked, flanking her from the other side. "What's wrong?"

"It's nothing," Liz said, louder. "It's just . . . I keep thinking about what Knight told you—about what the Circle is doing. . . . I don't know. It's just . . ." She gave a slight glance toward the window. "I can't help but worry that things are going to get worse before they get better."

Instinctively, my gaze followed hers. I totally knew the feeling.

It wasn't exactly surprising when I couldn't fall asleep. I thought about Liz's words, about my mother's warnings. Living to see graduation didn't seem as unlikely as it had a few months before, but Bex was right. The future was out there. And I couldn't shake the feeling that it was more than a little bit scary.

That was why I slipped out of my bed and out of our room, into the dark and chilly halls, wandering in silence until—

"Hi, Cammie."

The girl in the hall was tiny. Her arms and hands were so small, she looked almost like a doll; but her big brown eyes were so brilliant that I was convinced she had to be either dream or ghost.

"Sorry if I scared you," the girl told me. "I didn't know anyone else was up."

"That's . . . that's okay."

"You don't know me, do you?" the girl guessed. Then she shrugged and smiled a little. "That's cool." She honestly sounded like she meant it. "I'm Amy." She held out her hand in a manner that would have made Madame Dabney proud.

There was nothing at all self-conscious about her. She was so poised. So beautiful. If I hadn't known better, I might have thought that I had been transported back in time to an audience with a very tiny Cleopatra.

I studied the girl, wondering why—in that moment—she seemed so familiar. Probably I'd seen her around, encoded her face. Maybe I'd even met her last semester during one of the trances that had taken me out of my right mind. But in any case, it felt like I knew her when she asked, "Are you okay, Cammie?"

She tilted her head and looked up at me with those big, brown eyes. I wasn't surprised that she knew my name and my face. She'd probably heard more than a few stories about all that had happened in the past few years. And right then she was looking up to me. Literally. Figuratively. She was looking at me like I was exactly who she was hoping to grow up to be.

But right then all I wanted to do was go back in time and be her.

"I'm sorry," I told her. "I didn't recognize you."

"I'm a seventh grader." She shook her head slowly. "You're a senior. You're not supposed to recognize me. Besides, I thought I was coming to a school where not being recognizable was an advantage."

She laughed a little, completely at home and at ease, and even though I didn't know that seventh grader, I liked her.

"So tell me, Amy, what are you doing wandering around out here when everybody else is sleeping?"

"I like the mansion at night. It doesn't really feel like a school then. When I'm alone and barefoot on the carpets, it feels just like a home. Like my home."

I smiled and nodded and knew exactly what she meant.

The grandfather clock at the end of the hall started to chime. Three o'clock. In four hours, those halls would be filled with screaming girls and swinging backpacks, long lines at the waffle bar and a whole new semester.

My last semester.

I looked at my new little friend and tried to see the mansion through her eyes—before the world got so close to our walls.

"Good night, Cammie," Amy called to me as she walked

to the end of the hall. She stopped with her hand on the banister, looking back over her shoulder at me. "We're all glad you're back."

And then she disappeared up the stairs without a word or a sound; and I stood, silently wondering if I might have been mistaken. Maybe she really had been a dream.

Chapter Six

If our teachers were feeling any nostalgia about its being our Last First Day of a New Semester Ever, they totally didn't show it the following morning.

For starters, they made us have our breakfast conversations in Mandarin, and then Madame Dabney came by and reminded everybody that our holiday thank-you cards were due in the mail by noon. (Madame Dabney takes her thank-you cards very seriously.)

But the day didn't really get weird until my roommates and I joined the rest of the senior Covert Operations class in Sublevel Three. Because . . . well . . . Sublevel Three was empty.

Mr. Solomon was gone.

Aunt Abby was who-knew-where.

Technically, Agent Townsend hadn't been on the Gallagher Academy payroll all year.

Exactly who I had been expecting as soon as we stepped off the elevator and into the ancient space, I wasn't quite sure.

And then I heard the voices.

"Is the landline secure?" Mr. Smith asked.

"I think so," my mother said. "But needless to say, we aren't taking any chances."

"Ask for Romero," Mr. Smith was whispering just as the entire senior CoveOps class came walking around the corner.

"Mom?" I asked. "What are you doing here? Are you teaching us?" I asked, too much optimism in my voice. I should have known better.

"No, Cam. I'm sorry." Mom brushed a hand across my cheek and put something in a backpack.

Behind her, Mr. Smith closed a door marked STORAGE with a snap. I heard the whining of gears and motors as the school's security measures clicked into place, locking the closet, keeping whatever lay inside just out of reach.

"Good morning, ladies," Mr. Smith said, even though he'd already seen us in Countries of the World. "If you'll go back to class and take a seat, I'll be right—yes, Ms. McHenry?" he asked Macey with a sigh.

"Where's Mr. Solomon?"

"Away," Mr. Smith said in a manner that totally didn't encourage follow-up questions.

I watched the rest of the senior class pivot and start for our classroom, turning and moving like a flock of geese, but I was frozen to the spot. I looked from my mother to the backpack, from Mr. Smith's eyes to hers. And I knew what had brought her all the way to Sublevel Three.

"You found another descendant, didn't you?" I asked as

soon as the rest of the class had left, but I didn't wait for an answer. "Which one is it? William Smith? Is it the granddaughter in Toronto? I thought she might—"

"It's not the woman in Toronto," Mom said, her voice firm. "She's descended from a *different* William Smith. Now, you need to—"

"Don't tell me to stop worrying!" I snapped, louder than I'd intended. "The Circle of Cavan is planning something awful. Mr. Solomon and Zach are gone who knows where. We haven't seen Aunt Abby or Agent Townsend in weeks."

"Trust me, Cam, you don't need to worry about my sister and Agent Townsend," Mom said, but I was still rambling on.

"Zach's mother is going around killing people. She's killing people—*and their kids*—and I can't do anything but worry."

"I'm so sorry, sweetheart." Mom sounded like she meant it, and I think she really did. "I have to go."

I didn't ask where. I didn't ask why. I knew better than to beg for answers. She was never going to give them.

"Are you going to get Preston?" Macey called from the end of the hall.

Mom shook her head. "No."

"But you're leaving, aren't you? To track down one of them . . . one of the Inner Circle?" I asked, but my mother's silence was her answer.

I watched her turn and walk steadily to the end of the hall, no hesitation. No fear.

"Mom," I yelled, and she glanced back, dark hair falling across her shoulders. "Be careful."

* * *

It was cold as we walked from the P&E barn and back to the mansion that night. We shivered in our uniforms and thin sweaters. Overhead, there was a blanket of clouds hanging between us and a starry sky. I thought about Zach and Mr. Solomon, my mom and Aunt Abby. I wondered where in the world they might be. Was it cold there too? Or were they someplace where it was summer and the middle of the day? There were about a million things I didn't know, so I gave up trying to guess the answers. Instead, I wondered what they would do if they were the ones being left behind, treated like they were helpless.

The Circle of Cavan wasn't my own private mission, no matter how personal it felt. It hadn't started with me. But somehow I couldn't shake the feeling that it was going to end with me. Eventually.

And right then I couldn't take it anymore. The waiting. The helplessness. I didn't want to go back in time anymore. I was ready for my future when I stopped and asked, "Okay. What can we do?"

It wasn't a rhetorical question. Very few questions at our school ever are.

"What do you mean, Cam?" Liz asked.

"I mean, we don't know what the Inner Circle is planning and, aside from Ambassador Winters, we don't know where any of them are." I shrugged at the irony. "I don't even know where my boyfriend is. Still, I don't know about you guys, but I'm going to go crazy if I don't *do something.*"

Macey rolled her eyes. "I know. Let's stand around talking about it some more." Then she started toward the doors with new fire, new purpose. "No. I'm through talking."

"What are you doing, Mace?" Bex asked, blocking her way; but Macey didn't even look at her.

"What do you think I'm doing? I'm going to do what someone should have done weeks ago. I'm getting Preston out of there."

"Come on, Macey," Liz said. "Let's think about this."

"I'm *through* thinking."

"They said we shouldn't go, Macey." I took her arm, held her there. "They said he's not in any danger."

Macey gave a knowing—almost spiteful—smile. "And they'd never lie, would they?"

It only took a second for the words to seep in, and yet it seemed like it took forever. Of course my mother would lie. To keep me safe. To protect the mission. To stop the Circle and its leaders once and for all.

"I'm going to Rome," Macey told us. "Now, you can stay here or you can come with me. I'm not giving you a third option."

She turned and started inside, but in a flash, Bex's hand was on her arm, gently tugging her back as if pulling her away from a cliff.

Macey whirled on her. I wasn't sure if she was going to strike or just pull away; but she didn't have to do either because Bex was smiling, saying, "Then I guess we're going to miss some classes."

Chapter Seven

How to Sneak Out of Your School and
Cross the Atlantic Without a Whole
Bunch of Spies Being the Wiser:
(A list by Cameron Morgan)

- Secret passageways. I know I've mentioned these before, but seriously. My academic experience would have been extremely different without them.

- Roommates with private jets. Again, this makes things *a lot* easier. I'm not saying that we couldn't have stowed away on a cargo ship (that was Bex's original idea), but when Macey made a phone call and said, "The jet will be here in twenty," we didn't exactly protest.

- Don't go where you're going. No. Really. So you want to go to Rome to break out your roommate's boyfriend . . . the last thing you do is fly *to* Rome. Too obvious. Too easy to track. And, besides, we were in Macey's mom's private jet. There were going to be flight plans and manifests and stuff. So Rome was absolutely not our destination.

- Pack carefully (because even a rolling bag can be inconvenient in a high-speed chase, especially one involving cobblestones).

- Be careful.

————

The shoreline of Marseille was beautiful, I had to give it that much. I stood on the deck of the tiny boat that Macey had hired to take us across the Mediterranean, watching the lights disappear in the distance. Ocean spray slapped me in the face, and I had to keep hold of the railing to stay on my feet. Big swells rocked against the hull. A storm was moving in. That's when I felt the dark figure that came to stand beside me.

"Have you talked to Preston?" I asked Macey.

"Before we left for break your mother absolutely forbade me to speak to him. Remember?" she asked me.

"I do remember. So"—I looked at her from the corner of my eye—"what did he say?"

Another big wave crashed against the boat. Liz was down below, curled up in a little ball, eating green apples and every kind of anti-nausea medication we were able to smuggle out of the school's medical wing. Bex wasn't going to leave her, so that meant Macey and I were alone.

"He doesn't have a clue, Cam." She leaned her arms against the rail and stared out at the water, which was as blue as her eyes. "I called him on New Year's Eve. He was going to a party. He was . . . fine. That same day, Zach's mom was murdering a man and blowing up Cambridge, and Preston was talking about spring break. He asked me to come visit." Macey looked down at the water. "I think he really likes me."

"Of course he likes you."

"No." Macey shook her head. "I mean . . . he doesn't like *this*." Macey gestured down at her long legs and designer boots. The tight jeans and cashmere sweater. Even on a rickety boat in the middle of nowhere, she looked like she was at a photo shoot, but that didn't matter to Macey. Turns out, I guess, it didn't matter to Preston either.

"He likes *me*."

Maybe it's a spy thing, or maybe it's a girl thing—but when you spend your whole life trying out a series of aliases, it is a great comfort to find someone who knows and likes the person behind the cover.

"You know his schedule?" I asked.

"Some of it," Macey said.

"Good. When we get in there tomorrow . . . we're going to have to be careful."

"I know."

"We can't just walk up and grab him. His dad has to know what is going on—what Zach's mom is up to. He has to know he's a target. Which means Preston is going to have guards. And those guards are going to do everything they can to keep him away from the likes of us."

"I know." I could hear the annoyance in Macey's voice, but those things had to be said, and so I took it upon myself to say them.

"It's not going to be like it was last fall is what I'm saying. We can't knock on the embassy door and ask if Preston can come out and play. Well . . . we can if we want his dad to try to kill me again."

"I get it, okay?" Macey wasn't snapping, but she was frayed. I could hear it in her voice, see it in her eyes.

"I know you get it. It's just that this is serious, Macey. We might make things worse. In our business, there's always the chance that you are just going to make things worse. If we go in there without knowing exactly what we're doing, then people could get hurt. People could die. Are you willing to take that risk?"

"I know there are risks, Cammie. Okay? I know what's happening to him and around him . . . what the situation is and . . ." She trailed off. For a moment I thought she wouldn't even finish, but the she turned her gaze out to the water. "That's why I wish this boat would go faster."

Chapter eight

The street outside the ambassador's residence was quiet. Out front, marines stood guard by the gates. The lines of tourists and people needing visas stretched from the front doors and around the corner, waiting for the offices to officially open, but the four of us had just arrived at our post. It was easy to agree there was no use in trying to sleep.

"What do you think?" Bex asked me.

"It looks the same," I said from my place by the window. A steaming cup of hot cappuccino was in my hands, but I didn't sip. It was enough just to feel the warmth.

"That's good, isn't it?" Liz asked. "I mean, maybe it won't be so hard."

Macey cut her eyes at her. "Looks can be deceiving."

———

Covert Operations Report

The Operatives took up a position in a safe flat (*i.e.*, hotel room) overlooking the United States Embassy in Rome. They began taking shifts, keeping watch.

Over the course of eight hours the Operatives noticed five guard changes and the entrance of two motorcades. They also consumed a total of twelve cups of gelato.

The Operatives also observed a variety of strange patterns in the area:

Two unmarked vans kept a constant rotation outside the embassy's east gate.

Three separate tourists seemed to be more interested in getting pictures of embassy security than any of the traditional sights.

The Operatives also regretted not packing warmer sweaters.

"So what do we see?" Bex asked through my comms unit later that day. She and Liz were in a van, checking out the surrounding streets, scouring for a weakness in the embassy's defenses. But Macey was beside me, binoculars pressed against her eyes as we stared down at the embassy's front gates, watching. Counting.

"Anything going on?" Bex went on.

"Same old, same—wait," I said when the embassy's front

doors opened and two bodyguards walked out, a smaller, thinner figure with a backpack pressed between them.

"Is that . . . ?" I asked.

"It's him," Macey said. I felt her start to bolt, but then she stopped herself. Macey had come way too far to be stupid.

I watched Preston and his guards walk toward a waiting car and climb inside. The gates opened and, with a roar, two motorcycles pulled up to flank the limo as the three vehicles moved through the gates.

I knew part of Macey still wanted to run. But me . . . I was stunned, trapped in the memory of the men last fall who had chased me through the streets of Rome, and I knew that the men on the motorcycles weren't a part of the embassy's protective detail. They were Circle. And they were watching Preston's every move.

Just then one of the unmarked vans that had been rotating in and out of position on the street pulled into traffic, following Preston and his watchers into the distance.

"Cam?" I heard Bex's voice in my ear. "Cam, what's happening?"

"Bex, Liz," I said. "You'd better get back here. I think we need to hurry."

The school must have been a church once upon a time. At least part of it. The main hall had stained glass windows and a high, arching ceiling covered in mosaics. It was beautiful. Fortunately, its security was also totally lax.

The lock on the alley door was easy to pick. The back stairwell had no cameras. And, perhaps most importantly, the school's intercom system was incredibly hackable.

"Preston Winters, you are needed in room 84," the female voice on the intercom said.

That room 84 was the boys' bathroom, no one seemed to notice.

"Hey, stranger," Macey said, and Preston slammed the bathroom door behind him.

"Macey? What are you . . . I . . . I mean, you're in Rome. And you're in the boys' bathroom." He sounded like he wasn't certain which was more peculiar.

"I need to talk to you," she said, and I stayed quiet.

"It's so good to see you!" He stepped toward her. I think he was going to hug her—maybe kiss her. I kind of wanted to hide. But more than that, I wanted to get out of there.

Preston, on the other hand, seemed immune to the weirdness.

"Are you in town long?" he asked. "Where are you guys staying? Have you been to the embassy yet? Maybe we can—"

"We can't go to the embassy, Preston." Macey's voice was even. "You can never go back to the embassy again."

Then, for the first time, he looked at me. It was a look that said he thought it might be a joke, that she was teasing. Or just being a crazy politician's daughter. But Macey was through rebelling, and deep down Preston knew it. "Cammie?" he asked.

"It's complicated, Preston."

"Complicated . . . how?" he asked. His expression grew grave. "*Circle* complicated?"

"Yeah. We'll tell you all about it in a little—"

"Are you okay?" Terror filled his eyes. Last summer, he'd been the one I'd gone to when I was on the run. He'd taken me in and given me shelter. He knew what the Circle of Cavan was, but as far as we knew, he had no idea that his father was actually one of the Circle's leaders—that someday that job was supposed to pass to him.

"I'm okay. I'm safe. But you aren't." I stole a glance out the window. I didn't see Bex and Liz, but they were out there. Waiting. Ready. "Look, we don't have time to explain it all now, but we need you to trust us."

"Macey?" He turned to her just as there was a honk in the alley behind the school. Down below, we saw a truck moving to block the narrow passage. Vendors yelled. People on Vespas tried to squeeze around. But the truck didn't budge.

"Look, Preston, I wish we could explain everything. But we can't. Not yet. Bex and Liz are outside waiting for us, and we have to go. Now."

He glanced around, bewildered. "Where are they?"

Just then the truck honked again, as if in answer.

"That's a bread truck," Preston said, glancing out the window. "You came here in a bread truck?"

"Do you trust us?" Macey asked. It was the million-dollar question. Without the right answer, everything would have been for nothing.

Preston grinned. "Yes."

I reached for the window. "Then let's go."

I was unlatching the glass when I noticed Preston was no longer beside us.

There was a banging on the door. A deep voice was yelling, "Mr. Winters? Mr. Winters, open the door, sir." And Preston was halfway there.

"No!" Macey yelled and bolted across the room. She pressed his body against the door, and it looked like Preston couldn't decide whether to be worried or incredibly happy about the situation.

"Just you," she explained.

On the other side of the door, the guards banged again. I thought of the men on the motorcycles who had chased me through the streets last fall. Maybe they were the same ones who were in the hallway right then. Maybe this time I wasn't meant to get away so easily.

"They're my bodyguards," Preston tried to explain, but Macey just jerked him by the collar.

"You have new guards now," she said.

Preston, however, didn't look so sure.

"My dad said I should never go anywhere without them. There have been a few attacks against some high-profile people in Europe. Not that I'm all that important or anything," he tried to explain.

"Yeah, well, trust me. You're high-profile enough," I said. "That's kind of why we're here."

Down below, Bex honked again.

Outside, the banging grew louder. They were trying to break down the door.

"It's now or never, Preston," Macey told him, but he just looked at me.

"I came to you once, Preston," I said. "When I had nowhere else to go. I was hurt and bleeding and scared, and you saved me. You saved my life. Now I'm trying to return the favor."

He turned to Macey then, reaching out to take her hand. And together they climbed onto the windowsill.

And jumped.

Chapter nine

We were almost to the end of the alley when we heard the explosion. The truck shook. Macey was knocked off her feet, and Bex put the pedal to the metal, laying rubber down the cobblestone alley. When we reached the street, she didn't even slow down. We shot into traffic, tires squealing, while black smoke filled the air behind us.

"Uh . . ." Terror filled Preston's eyes. "I think my school is on fire."

"We know," Macey said.

His eyes got even wider. "*How* do you know?"

"Because we're the ones who set it," Macey said as if it were the most obvious thing in the world; but Preston just looked at us all in turn, taking it in. He knew the truth about the Gallagher Academy, after all. He shouldn't have been surprised. But I guess there are some things you have to see to believe, and it was like Preston was seeing us for the very first time.

"Oh," he said numbly. "Okay."

In the front seat, Liz spun around. She had a laptop open and yelled at me, "He's transmitting!" Then she looked at the boy and smiled. "Hi, Preston!"

"Hi, Liz. How are you—hey—hey!"

He stopped talking. I'm pretty sure that's what most boys would do if Macey McHenry were ripping off their shirts.

"Macey!" Preston gasped, but Macey didn't slow down.

"Take it off," she told him. "Take it all off."

She had ripped the button-down shirt off his arms and was going to work on his belt.

"No," Preston snapped. But he didn't protest long because, if I'm going to be honest—which is kind of the point of these reports—I was already unzipping his pants.

Then Macey started ripping off Preston's white T-shirt. (Yes, actual *rippage*.) And I was fighting with his zipper. I wasn't exactly proud of how we handled the situation, but desperate times call for incredibly desperate measures.

"Give me everything you have," I told him.

"Really, Cammie. I never knew you thought of me that way."

Preston's pants were undone by that point and I ordered, "Step!"

He did as he was told, and a moment later I had the pants in my hands.

Preston just stood there, dumbfounded, in his boxers as I cracked open the back of the truck and hurled the pants into the street. A split second later the rest of his clothes and shoes followed.

"Hey!" he shouted, but right then, through the open doors,

I heard the roar of motorcycles. Memory came rushing back. Terror mixed with adrenaline, and I didn't feel sorry for the mostly naked boy. Not even a little bit. I just wanted us all to get out of this alive.

"Liz?" Macey asked, but Liz shook her head. "No go," she said. "He's still got a signal."

"What if it's *in* him?" Macey asked.

"Then we cut it out," I said, pressing Preston to the floor of the moving truck.

"I don't like the sound of this!" Preston shouted, his voice way more high-pitched than any eighteen-year-old guy ever wants his voice to be, but I didn't have time to care. I was looking at his body, examining every inch for scars.

"Have you had any shots, Preston? Any implants in the last six months?"

"What?" he shouted.

"Focus," Macey said. I thought she was going to slap him.

"I . . . I had to go to the dentist!" he shouted.

I didn't ask for an invitation. I pried open his mouth like Grandpa Morgan trying to buy a horse.

"Retainer," I told Macey.

"Give it to us, Preston," she told him.

"No." He scooted farther back, pressing against the side of the truck.

"Give it to us," I told him. "Or I borrow Bex's knife."

And that must have done it, because he handed me the slimy piece of plastic and metal. I hurled it out the back of the van.

And we waited.

Seconds stretched out for what seemed like hours before Liz finally gave the longest sigh I'd ever heard.

"That does it," she said. "He's clean."

Only then did Macey and I drop to the floor of the truck. Breathing hard. Hearts pounding. I laid my head against a basket full of croissants, resting there, staring at Preston, who sat in his boxer shorts, arms crossed self-consciously across his chest.

"Are you going to explain?" Preston was trying to keep his voice steady and failing. "What is going on?"

I wanted to tell him everything—about his father and Zach's mother and all the ways his life was getting ready to change, but I couldn't say a word because Bex was already yelling, "Hang on!"

Rebecca Baxter may possibly be the greatest spy I'll ever know. She's also probably the most aggressive driver. So when she gripped the wheel and took a corner far faster than any bread truck is ever supposed to move, we all held on for dear life while the truck jumped the curb and burst through a newsstand.

Preston looked like he might throw up, and I couldn't really blame him.

Liz turned around and handed a bundle of clothes between the seats. "Here you go," she said.

"You brought clothes?" Preston asked. "You knew you were going to make me jump out of a window. And strip. And throw a perfectly good retainer away?"

Bex glanced back. "I was just hoping about the stripping part. Nice abs, by the way." Then she went back to driving.

"Look, Preston," Macey started. "We can explain. And we will. Soon. But right now we have to get you someplace safe."

"I *was* someplace safe! And then you made me jump out a window and blew up my school!"

"You *weren't* someplace safe," Macey told him just as I heard the roar.

"And, technically, we didn't blow up the school," Liz qualified. "It was a very small and highly controlled explosion."

Through the dirty windows at the back of the truck, I saw motorcycles come racing up behind us. I felt Bex jerk the wheel, and the truck skidded onto a main street, going in the wrong direction.

Cars honked. Pedestrians yelled as Bex swerved onto the sidewalk. But still she didn't slow down.

Preston's breath was coming harder than it should have as he asked, "What is going on?"

Before I could explain Bex said, "Guys, we have—"

But she never got to finish. The crash came too fast—too hard. One second we were careening along the Roman streets, and the next there was nothing but the screech of tires and the crunch of metal. I felt myself falling, tumbling in the back of the truck as it flipped onto its side. Sparks and scraping metal. Something was pushing us across the street.

And then we were falling, tumbling over and over like clothes in a dryer, until there was a splash and then nothing but cold and fear.

* * *

The river was freezing. Bread floated all around us as the water cascaded through the back of the truck and the broken windows, taking us lower. Deeper into the cold.

"Preston!" Macey was yelling, but she sounded too far away. "Preston!" she called again.

Slowly, water filled the back of the truck, and as my eyes adjusted to the black, my head swirled. Blood ran down my face. I wanted to be sick or maybe just close my eyes and sleep, but then I thought about what I'd told Bex just days before: what I really wanted to be was alive.

So I kicked and clawed and swam toward the broken doors at the back of the truck, and that was when I saw him. Preston's eyes were closed and his lips were turning blue. A bump was growing on his head, and I knew it wasn't just the cold water that was sending him into shock.

"Preston! Cam!" Macey yelled again, and I realized it was coming through my earpiece.

"I've got him," I yelled. "Swim!" I ordered, and put my head down, pulling Preston out of the truck as quickly as I could. My friends must have done as I said, because when I surfaced they were gone.

Air bubbled up from the sinking truck.

"Cammie!" Liz yelled. She sounded afraid, but I couldn't see her. It was like I was in an echo chamber. The whole world had had the volume turned down.

"Cammie, are you okay?" Liz said just as a bullet pierced the water, slicing into the murky darkness. *Splash*. And then another. And another.

So I just put my head down and kept on swimming, dragging Preston toward the shore.

The current must have carried us farther away from the wreckage than I realized, because when Preston and I came up for air, I gasped and looked around—waiting—but no shots came.

In the distance, there was shouting.

"Cammie?" Preston said, his voice groggy. "What happened? Where am I?"

"We went for a little swim, Pres. And now we've got to go for a run."

"I don't feel so good."

"I know, but you can do it. Come on. I'll help you."

Running down the streets of Rome, I didn't dare stop to think about what we must have looked like. A tiny line of blood was smeared across Preston's face. My wet hair was tangled and filled with broken glass. Blood ran into my eyes, and the sweatshirt we'd packed for Preston was two sizes too big and hung off him like a wet blanket.

Macey and Bex and Liz were on the other side of the river, running past an SUV with a pair of busted headlights, and I immediately knew what had caused the crash. As they passed, the SUV revved its engine and started chasing after them, swerving in and out of traffic. Other cars stopped, but the SUV just kept coming, plowing onto sidewalks, bursting through barricades.

"Run!" Bex yelled, her voice carrying across the river, and Preston and I didn't have to be told twice.

I reached for Preston's hand, dragging him away. But the motorcycles were already weaving across a bridge, rushing toward us. I heard the haunting, piercing wails of police cars and fire trucks. In less than two minutes, our sinking truck would be surrounded by authorities. Cops and bystanders would fill the streets, searching.

The motorcycle engines revved.

We didn't have two minutes.

Preston's hand was too still. He was going into shock. Of course he was. He was human. He was just a boy, no matter who his father was. And I knew it was up to me to pull the ambassador's son away from the sirens and the sinking truck, the motorcycles and the men who wouldn't stop until they found us.

Preston was the asset. The Gallagher Girl part of me knew that getting him out of there was my job—my mission. "Let's go," I shouted.

"This way," Preston said. We were on his home turf, and I let him drag me into an alley I'd never seen before. Laundry hung on lines overhead, blocking out the sun. And still we ran faster and faster, pushing aside the low-hanging sheets that floated around us like ghosts. And then we broke free of the alley and onto another street, light streaming all around us, and I knew where Preston was going.

"Is that the embassy?" I asked, already sure of the answer.

"Yeah. We're almost there."

Even drenched and freezing, shocked and terrified, Preston was stronger than he looked. It was all I could do to stop him.

"No!" I shouted, jerking his arm, pulling him out of the street.

"Cam, we'll be safe at the embassy. It's US soil. They can't get us."

"No, Preston." I shook my head. I found his eyes. I had to make him see—make him understand. But not even the Gallagher Academy can teach you how to change somebody's world, alter everything they'd ever thought was true.

"What aren't you telling me?" he shouted. It went far beyond fear and rage and panic. Preston was desperate. And desperate people do desperate things. "It's the Circle, isn't it? They're after us."

"Yes."

"Is it because of last summer? Because you stayed here? Did you leave something or—"

"The Circle isn't after you, Preston. The Circle . . . it *is* you."

"What do you mean?"

"When did you get your new bodyguards? Was it back before Christmas?"

He didn't say a word, but the answer was written all over his face.

"A lot of strange things started happening then, didn't they?" I asked him. "Murders of prime ministers . . . disappearances of bigwigs in the European Union . . . Strange things keep happening to powerful people. People whose families have been powerful for centuries. People whose ancestors used to follow the teachings of a man named Iosef Cavan."

"No." Preston shook his head. He eased away from me.

"Think about it, Preston. Something has been different lately, hasn't it? Your dad, he's been changing his patterns. Fewer trips out of the embassy? New cars? New guards? New protocols?" I spoke slowly, but still Preston inched farther and farther away from me and the things I had to say. "Someone is hunting Circle members, Preston—the descendants of the Circle founders."

"No." Preston shook his head.

"Someone is hunting *you*."

Carefully, I reached into the pocket of my jeans, my cold hands scraping against the wet denim; but I clawed until I found the piece of paper. Gently, I unfolded it, peeling back the damp layers until I could look down at the names I knew by heart.

"This is why they wanted me, Preston. Because years ago I saw this list. Because I knew about the people who founded the Circle of Cavan. Look, Preston. Look!" I pointed to the names. "Elias Crane. His great-great-great-great grandson is dead. Charles Dubois's great-great-great-great granddaughter and her kids are probably dead. Look at the last name, Preston."

"No."

"Samuel is a family name, isn't it?" I asked. "Wasn't your dad named for a relative who fought in the Civil War?"

There was no denying the truth in what I'd said, but Preston just shook his head.

"So what if he was? That doesn't mean my family has anything to do with the Circle."

"Yes, Preston." I nodded. "That's exactly what it means."

"Dad!" Preston yelled. He gripped the iron fence, pleading. But the man only ran faster to the chopper and closed the door, blocking off the sound of Preston's cries.

"Dad?" Preston asked one final time. This time it wasn't a scream. It was a whimper.

Then the whole scene changed.

It was like the whole thing was happening in slow motion. I heard the sirens. I recognized the snipers for what they were the moment they appeared on the embassy's roof. What I didn't know was *why*.

The helicopter started to rise, but someone fired a warning shot and the chopper hovered.

More guards filled the courtyard, rifles trained on Preston's father. And when a voice came booming through a bullhorn, I knew.

"Samuel Winters, you are under arrest," Agent Townsend said. I saw him appear then, through the crowd. My aunt Abby stood at his side, her dark hair blowing in the swirling wind. "Land the chopper or we will fire. I repeat, we will fire."

"What . . . what's happening?" Preston asked, turning to me. "You brought them here." He glared.

"I didn't."

"That's your aunt, Cammie! I know you brought her here!" He pointed to where Agent Townsend was dragging Preston's father out of the helicopter and placing him in handcuffs.

"I didn't know they were coming. But I knew you were in danger," I said. "It will be okay, Preston. You have to trust me."

And maybe he would have. Maybe he would have believed

"You're wrong. You're *lying*."

"I'm not lying."

"My parents were nice to you. My dad helped you!"

"He tried to kill me, Preston. He would have killed me."

"You're a spy. You lie. It's what you do."

"I'm not lying now."

Preston continued to inch away from me—from the truth he no longer wanted to hear.

When a helicopter roared overhead and began to land in the courtyard inside the closed gates of the embassy, I looked away for a split second. I swear I didn't lose focus for more than a breath. But when I turned back, Preston was bolting into the street, into traffic, pushing people aside and running against the grain to the embassy's gates.

"Dad!" he yelled, and then I saw what he was seeing. Ambassador Winters was out of the building and walking across the courtyard. He crouched beneath the chopper's spinning blades and only stopped when his son's cries broke through the air.

"Dad! Wait! Open the gates," Preston yelled.

"Preston, stop," I called after him.

He stole a hurried, frantic glance in my direction, but ran even faster, as if he was no longer sure exactly who to trust. totally knew the feeling.

"Open the gates!" Preston yelled again, but the guards mu have been given some kind of order because they glanced at t ambassador and the gates stayed closed.

what I was saying—despite what he was seeing. Maybe everything would have made sense in a matter of time if Agent Townsend hadn't turned and started toward us, yelling, "Preston Winters?"

As soon as I heard Agent Townsend's voice, I felt a sense of relief. He'd help us get Preston home. He'd help us keep Preston safe.

"Where are they taking my father?" Preston asked, but he didn't rush the man. He was shaking too badly. I didn't know if it was the cold or the rage, but I guess it didn't matter.

Agent Townsend reached for Preston's trembling hands. "Mr. Winters, you are under arrest for the suspicion of espionage."

Townsend spun Preston around, pressing his body into the fence.

"No!" someone shouted. I saw Bex and Liz running toward us, neither of them able to keep up with Macey. They all had blankets draped over their shoulders, but Macey's blew free as she ran. She looked a lot like an angel losing her wings.

"Take him away," Townsend told another agent, but Macey was on him then.

"Stop," she yelled, trying to get to Preston. "He doesn't know anything."

"That is for us to determine, Ms. McHenry."

"You're wrong! You're making a mistake," she shouted.

Agent Townsend had been our teacher. He'd been our ally. Our confidant. Our friend. Sure, we'd never really *liked* him; but I'd grown fond of Agent Townsend. He was one of the good guys, but that didn't stop Macey's fists from beating against him.

She looked frail and feminine. She didn't fight like a Gallagher Girl right then. She fought like a girl who was watching the only boy who'd ever known and cared about the real her being dragged away. Maybe forever.

A pair of agents took Preston by each arm and led him to a white van that sat in the courtyard, lights spinning.

There was another van exactly like it not far away, and I could see the ambassador sitting in the back. The streets surrounding the embassy were on fire with lights and sirens and swarming crowds, but the ambassador looked only at me. He gave a nod in my direction as if to make sure I knew it wasn't over.

Then another man climbed into the back of the van and sat beside Preston's father. I recognized this new man, though it took me a moment to remember from where. The man's hair was slightly thinning. He had a normal build. A normal face. He could have been an accountant, an English teacher, a mid-level manager in any company in the world.

But he wasn't. He was Interpol. And when he brought a hand to his temple—a tip of the imaginary hat—I was quite certain that I would be seeing him again very, very soon.

When the agents closed the door and drove the man and Preston's father away, I looked down at the piece of paper that was still in my hands. The ink looked like blood, running across the page. Without a word, Liz handed me a pen, and I crossed off the name at the bottom of the list.

Four down.

Three to go.

Chapter Ten

We had dry clothes and hot coffee, but even as we sat on Macey's jet, I didn't feel any warmer. Or safer. In a few minutes, we'd take off. In a few hours, we'd be home. Preston was, technically, out of harm's way, but it still felt like our mission was a complete and utter failure.

Macey sat beside me, motionless. I wanted to tell her that it was okay, that Preston would be safe now. But Macey didn't want to hear it. Which was just as well. I didn't want to say it.

When the jet's door slid down and Aunt Abby stepped in, I thought that we were ready to go home. But then someone else climbed into the cabin.

"What are you doing here?" Macey shouted at Agent Townsend. "Where's Preston?"

Macey was up and moving toward him, and I could have sworn Agent Townsend looked scared.

"Macey." Abby blocked her way. "I'll be asking the questions.

Now, *sit down*," Abby ordered. And for once in her life, Macey did as she was told.

There was a bandage on Townsend's temple. "Are you okay?" I said.

"I will survive, Ms. Morgan. Thank you for asking."

"No," Abby snapped. "Cameron Ann Morgan, don't you sit there acting like you're so sorry. I'm not even going to ask the four of you why you're here. *I don't care.* What were you thinking—stumbling into a live op like that?" my aunt asked, but all I could think of was how she'd been when she first came to my school. Cocky and easy and fun. She'd grown up. And I guess she wasn't the only one.

Bex shifted in her seat. "We didn't know it was a live op."

"Well, you should have known." Abby had her hand on her hip. She sounded like my mother. "You all should have known better. You're seniors. You should realize by now that everything you do comes with repercussions."

"How were we supposed to know you'd be there?" Macey challenged. She crossed her long arms. "All anyone ever says is *Don't worry about Preston. Preston isn't in trouble. We won't let Preston get hurt.*"

"And we *didn't*," Abby countered. "We had eyes on the embassy at all times."

"So that you could take him!" Macey shouted, and, for that, not even Abby had an answer. She and Townsend shared a look and, I'm not going to lie, it kind of scared me. Macey must have seen it too, because her voice changed. Anger morphed to terror.

"Where is he?" she asked. "Where is he right now?"

Townsend shook his head slowly. He ran a hand through his hair and took a seat. I watched my aunt lean ever so slightly against him.

"We don't know, Ms. McHenry," he said.

"You're lying," Macey snapped.

"We would lie—if we had to. But we aren't," Abby said with a shake of her head. "All Circle operatives are held in a high-security facility, the location of which is need-to-know, and *we don't know*. I can promise you that."

"I don't believe you," Macey told her.

"That's fine." Abby shook her head. "But I'm telling you the truth. He'll be okay, Macey. It's normal. It's protocol."

"Protocol for what?" Bex asked.

"He'll be questioned, along with his father," Townsend said.

"Questioned . . ." Macey started. "You mean, interrogated. You mean, *tortured*."

"He's in the authorities' hands, girls," Abby said. "He'll be fine."

"Like Cammie is fine," Macey said, then glanced at me. "No offense."

"None taken," I said. "I think."

"We aren't the Circle, Macey," Abby told her. "We're the good guys."

Macey crossed her arms. "Forgive me if I have my doubts."

"What about Preston's mother?" Liz asked.

"She'll be questioned too, I'm sure," Townsend said. "But the Circle doesn't exactly admit spouses, so I doubt she knows anything. She'll stay at the embassy for now."

"That man . . . in the van with Preston's father—" I said.

"His name is Max Edwards," Townsend filled in before I could say anything more. "He used to be with Interpol."

"I remember him. I met him two years ago at the career fair. He told me he knew my father." I thought about the man who had given me his business card during my sophomore year. He'd looked at me that night like he saw through my *chameleonness*. He'd looked at me that way again that afternoon. Something about it made me feel uneasy, vulnerable. Naked.

"I don't doubt it," Townsend said. "Edwards has been in this business a long time. He knows everyone. That's why he's heading up the task force."

"What *task force?*" Bex didn't even try to hide the skepticism in her voice.

"Seems the intelligence community is finally starting to take the list seriously, girls," my aunt told us. "Edwards is in charge of a brand-new task force that has just been put in place. It's not big. Just a few key agents from the CIA, MI6, all the usual suspects. They're supposed to track down the Inner Circle. Not that it's going to be easy. But they're going to try. And if today is any indication, they might just succeed. Winters is the first Inner Circle member to be taken alive, after all."

Knowing what we knew about the Circle's network of moles within the world's intelligence community, I started to agree. Maybe it would work. Maybe we wouldn't have to be alone in the search anymore. But Macey just crossed her arms and huffed.

"You mean the Inner Circle and their families?" she asked.

"Preston needed to be questioned, ladies," Agent Townsend said as if he expected that to be the end of it.

"But . . ." Liz spoke then. Her voice cracked. "He's just a kid."

"You don't get it, do you?" Abby leaned forward, staring at the four of us as if she were about to give us the most important lesson of our covert lives. "You should stop and listen to yourselves sometime. 'We're *practically adults*, let us run wild.' 'We're *only kids*, leave us alone.'" I watched my aunt lean closer, emphasize every word. "*You can't have it both ways.*"

"When is Preston's birthday, Macey?" Townsend asked.

"December fifth," Macey said.

"Then he just turned eighteen, did he not?"

"So what?"

"So he's an adult now, by our standards. And the Circle's." Townsend looked at us all as if part of him truly hated what he had to say. "So no matter what we know about his father's dealings, at this moment, there is a good possibility that Preston knows more."

Macey was shaking her head. "No. No. He didn't know a thing."

"Didn't he?" Townsend asked. "Abby is right. You want to be treated like grown-ups? Well, that includes both the good and the bad. And the possibility exists, ladies, that Preston Winters might be very bad indeed."

My roommates and I fell into silence. I didn't say a thing because, like it or not, the adults in my life were right far more often than they were wrong.

The Circle had always been a step or two ahead—and right then, I didn't like where those steps were going.

Chapter ELEVEN

It was dark when the jet finally landed. I'm sure I must have slept on the long ride over the Atlantic, but I don't really remember. I just remember staring out the window: watching, thinking, waiting for something, but what, I didn't know.

On the Tarmac, Agent Townsend whispered something to Abby, then squeezed her hand and kissed her softly when he didn't think we were watching. But we're Gallagher Girls. To tell you the truth, we are always watching.

Abby let him go, her eyes a little misty. And I couldn't help myself—I thought about Zach. He was out in the world somewhere. And a part of me worried that I might never see him again.

"Go to bed, girls," Abby told us when we walked through the doors. The lights were out. Our school was sleeping, and in the stillness I could feel how far we'd gone, and how far we still had to go.

"But—"

"I'm not going to tell you again," Abby snapped, and started down the hall that led to the stairs to the teachers' quarters. "Now go to bed."

And maybe we would have done exactly that, except when we reached the top of the Grand Stairs, I saw the light seeping from underneath my mother's office door, and that was all the invitation I needed. I raced down the Hall of History and never looked back.

"Mom!" I yelled. "Mom, I'm—" I said, bursting through the door; but then I stopped cold because Joe Solomon was lying on the leather couch in my mother's office. And, oh yeah, his shirt was totally off.

"Uh . . ." I said. I might have physically stumbled. But what else was I supposed to do at the sight of my teacher—and my mom's new sort-of boyfriend—*with his shirt off*?

It was epic. It was awkward. It was epically awkward.

And judging from the traffic jam of girls who were plowing into me from behind, I totally wasn't the only one who thought so.

"Uh . . ." Liz echoed me but couldn't find the words to finish, either.

"I'm fine," Mr. Solomon said, and then he tried to sit upright. I could see the bruises that covered his chest, spreading across his ribs. When he shifted on the sofa, I saw the massive gash in his side, and I felt the cold feeling of dread that maybe he wasn't the only one who'd gotten hurt.

"Where's Zach?" I blurted.

"He's fine," Mr. Solomon said, even though, technically, he hadn't answered my question.

"Step aside, girls," my mother said from behind us, and we moved out of the doorway and into the office, watched her dip a sponge into a bowl of sudsy water and kneel at Mr. Solomon's feet. He winced when she brought the sponge to the long, ragged knife wound that ran across his ribs.

"Wimp," she told him. He smiled.

"Did you find Catherine?" Bex blurted. "Did she do that to you?"

"No." Mr. Solomon shook his head. He sounded more disappointed than pained, like he'd gladly suffer a thousand cuts if it meant bringing Zach's mother to her end.

"Where is Zach?" I asked. "Is he . . ." I trailed off. I just looked at Mr. Solomon's blood and couldn't finish.

"Go to bed, girls," Mom said, but she didn't look at me. "I will deal with you in the morning."

"But—" Liz started.

"But nothing." Mom never took her eyes off of Joe Solomon. He winced again when she started wrapping a bandage tighter and tighter around his ribs.

"The hospital staff should be doing this," she told him.

Mr. Solomon smiled. "I like the nurse I've got."

"Girls, I need to debrief Mr. Solomon, and he needs to visit the hospital wing."

"No, he doesn't," Mr. Solomon said, but Mom gave him her "mom" look, and he backed down.

"He's going to tell me about his mission, and then he's going to have his head CAT scanned and his ribs X-rayed. I will talk to you girls in the morning." She ushered us toward the door. "It will all be better tomorrow."

I wanted to think it was true—that my mother was right, and that there was nothing a night in my own bed would not fix. But I wasn't so certain. Especially when we walked into the suite and saw that someone was already sleeping in my bed.

"Zach!" I didn't care that I was yelling. I ran to him. He propped himself up on one elbow and gave me a sleepy smile.

"You woke me," he said.

"You're not supposed to be in this part of the school," I said.

He took my hand, held it against his chest, and said, "Spy."

"Hello, Zachary." Bex was sauntering through the door. "It's nice to see you. Now, get out."

He didn't have to be told twice. He pushed himself off the bed and started for the door, pulling me along behind him.

We didn't say a word as we crept down the hall lined with suites filled with sleeping girls. Neither of us spoke when we reached the spiraling staircase at the back of the school.

The stone was cold against my skin. A freezing wind blew through the cracks in the old windows. But Zach's hand was warm in mine, and I didn't feel the chill, even when he stopped me on the stairs, pressed me against the wall, and kissed me. Softly at first, then more urgently, hungrily. It was like he hadn't eaten in weeks.

"Hi," he said finally, pulling back and running his hands through my hair.

"Hi," I said and kissed him again. I didn't think about the classes I'd missed or the ones that would be waiting on me in just a few hours. I couldn't even dream of going to bed.

"You were gone," I whispered into his skin. "You were gone for so long."

"I'm back now."

"Don't go again," I told him, but he said nothing. That was the kind of promise that spies could never make, so he just took my hand and led me farther down the stairs, into the wide corridor that ran along the back of the school.

"You saw Preston?" he asked when we reached the warmth of the hall.

I nodded.

"And they took him?"

Again, I couldn't say the words but didn't have to.

"Where were you, Zach?"

"Looking" was his answer.

"For your mom?" My voice cracked, but I didn't hide it.

"We didn't find her."

"She found us. In Cambridge. She killed Walter Knight." I made myself look at him, see the hurt that filled his eyes. He already knew about our mission, of course. But I had to say it anyway. I had to be the one to tell him, even if he wasn't hearing it for the first time.

"I'm so sorry. If she hurt you . . ." He ran his hand along

my neck and shifted my head, as if to make sure everything was the way it should be.

"I'm fine."

"I'll kill her."

"Don't say that, Zach."

"But I will, Cammie." He pulled away from me then, as if he couldn't bear to touch me with his hands—dirty hands. Like I deserved better than to be touched by the hands of a killer. "Someday. I will."

"No." I reached for him.

"Yes." His voice was sad, not cocky. It was like he'd seen the future, and he was finally telling me the thing he'd always known, Zachary Goode's great and final secret. "I will."

"Where were you, Zach? What happened to Mr. Solomon? To you?"

Zach ran a hand through his hair. He was far too young to look so exhausted.

"You know how we started out tracking my mom. . . . Well, we figured the best way to find her would be to find whatever Circle descendant she had her sights set on next."

"Which one?" I asked.

"Delauhunt," Zach told me. "Frederick Delauhunt. He's an arms dealer. We tracked him down to this fortress outside of Buenos Aires. He probably had fifty armed guards. And we could tell by the activity in the compound that they were getting ready to move him. We should have waited for backup, but I kept thinking about what would happen if we didn't find him again. I thought about what they did to you. And then I got stupid." Zach took a deep breath. "And Joe got hurt."

He eased slowly away, almost like he was content to leave me, like deep down he knew that I was better off without him. "You should probably go to bed, Gallagher Girl."

"I'm not sleepy."

"You should go to bed anyway. Try to get some sleep."

I leaned into him. "No. I shouldn't." I took both his hands in mine and stepped backward. "Do you want to see something cool?"

"What do you think?" he asked with that roguish grin he'd first given me when he'd walked through our doors as an exchange student. Before things got complicated. Before his mother changed my life.

I walked to an old candelabra that the housekeeping staff rarely remembered to clean, so it was dusty when I reached for it. And pulled.

Slowly, a door opened a crack. "What is that?" Zach asked, creeping closer.

I took his hand again. "Come on."

There was a time when I loved being in the secret passageways on my own. I would slip inside the darkness and disappear, be alone in the middle of a hundred people, be myself inside a place where you spend most of your time learning to be somebody else.

I'd never shown that one to Bex. I'd never brought Liz or Macey there to study. That was my private passage, and as I held on to Zach's hand, it felt very much like it still was. Only then, it wasn't mine. It was ours.

We squeezed together through dusty corridors and tight shadowy spaces, skirting between decaying beams. It must have been the servants' quarters once upon a time, because there was a round window there in the narrow space. It stared out to the east, across the grounds and the hills and the trees.

We stood together, looking out at a world that was covered with frost, a shimmering white glow.

"Wow," Zach said. He pressed up against the window, which fogged with his breath.

Sometime years before, I had dragged an old bean bag chair to that place. I watched Zach sink onto it, and then he pulled me down to lean against him. I felt his arms go around me, holding me tight.

I was safe.

I was warm.

I was home.

Chapter twelve

PROS AND CONS OF THE WEEK
THAT FOLLOWED:

PRO: Nothing helps take your mind off of stumbling into (and almost messing up) a live CIA operation like makeup work.

CON: We had to do a lot of makeup work.

PRO: We no longer had to wonder whether or not Zach's mom was going to come after Preston at the embassy.

CON: We had no idea where Preston was.

PRO: Zach was back.

CON: I couldn't shake the feeling that it was just a matter of time until we all had to go away again.

———

I could tell you that the week that followed was a pretty typical week at the Gallagher Academy. I could tell you that, but I'd be lying. After all, my roommates and I were not just the girls who had missed the first few days of classes of the spring semester—we were also the girls who had been there when Ambassador Winters was taken into custody, which in teenage-spy-girl terms didn't make us famous. It made us *infamous*. And let me tell you, that is a really big distinction.

"So, Cam," Tina Walters said, slipping her arm through mine as we walked into the Grand Hall, "I heard that Winters is locked in an underwater facility off the coast of Greenland. What do you know about that?"

"Nothing, Tina," I said.

"But the cover story is bogus, right? I mean, I know they've told the press that he was extracted based on intel that he was going to be the target of a terror plot, but that's not true, is it?"

Tina leaned a little closer, studying me so intently I thought my skin might catch fire. I was sure she didn't actually know the truth. Very few people did. That's the thing about spies. Most of the secrets we keep are from each other.

I liked Tina.

I even trusted Tina.

But I couldn't tell Tina the truth. Not because she was the school gossip (even though she was), but because, from that point forward, almost everything about my life was on a need-to-know basis and, right then, Tina didn't. No matter how much she probably thought otherwise.

"So . . ." Tina asked slowly. "What's the deal?"

"I don't have a clue, Tina." I shook my head, and thought about the look the ambassador had given me as he sat in the back of the van, defiant. Had that look been a threat? A warning? Or maybe just a good-bye. I shook my head again and said, "I really don't know," realizing it wasn't even a lie.

"What I want to know," Courtney started, leaning into the conversation as we sat down at the senior table, "is what is the deal with *Preston* Winters . . . ?"

"He's cute," Anna Fetterman said, then blushed.

"Yeah," Tina agreed. "I'm sure he was really cute when they led him away in handcuffs."

Anna gasped. "They didn't?"

Tina nodded slowly. "They did. To tell you the truth, I always got the feeling he might be kind of evil. It's the dimples," she hurried to add. "I, for one, never trust a boy with dimples."

Macey bristled but didn't say a word. After that, the Grand Hall fell quiet. Or as quiet as the Grand Hall ever is. I wanted to grab Macey and pull her away, tell her that it was all going to be fine. That Tina and the CIA and MI6 and that man from Interpol were all wrong—that Preston wasn't like his father.

But just then, from across the table, Bex caught my eye, and I could tell she was thinking it too: *What if he is?*

"Cameron," Professor Buckingham's voice came slicing through the Grand Hall, "if you are finished with your breakfast, I need you to come with me, please."

"Why?" I bolted to my feet. "What's wrong?"

"Right this way, dear," Buckingham said. She swept her arm toward the big double doors, and I didn't have a choice. I followed.

* * *

"Hello, Cammie."

For a moment, I couldn't move—couldn't speak. I stood just inside my mother's office door looking at the man I'd last seen sitting in a van with Ambassador Winters in Rome. I remembered everything about him—the moment he'd given me his business card two years before as I snuck out of our school to see my first boyfriend; the look on his face two days before as they were driving Preston and his father away. I knew exactly who I'd been brought to see. What I couldn't imagine was why.

He seemed to doubt my memory, though, because he extended a hand.

"We met once—a long time ago. I'm Max—"

"Edwards," I filled in. "Formerly of Interpol. More recently of a high-level task force in charge of arresting high-level Circle leaders and their teenage sons."

He laughed a little, amused by my moxie, then said, "It's nice to see you again, Cammie. I'm sorry we didn't get to speak in Rome. I've become something of . . . a fan."

He had a way of speaking, low and almost under his breath, as if I were the only person in the world who was meant to hear his words, even as we stood three feet away from my mother.

"Oh. Really?" I said, almost mocking, as he looked at me over the top of his glasses.

"It's a compliment, Cammie. You've made quite a name for yourself, you know?"

I did know. But I was also pretty sure that it wasn't the kind of compliment *covert* operatives usually wanted.

He lowered his voice even further. "I was very sorry to hear about your father's passing. And what you went through. You have my condolences, Cammie."

But I didn't want his sympathy. So I just turned toward my mother. "What is he doing here?" I asked.

"He's here with a request," my mother said.

"As you are well aware, Cammie, the Circle of Cavan is currently engaged in a record level of activity," the man told me. "As such, there is a new interagency task force. CIA. MI6. Interpol. Israeli Secret Service. All the usual players are taking part, and—"

"I know all this. Get to the part I don't know," I told him, my patience running out.

"What you saw in Italy, Cammie. That was the result of this task force. We're going to track the Circle leaders down."

I glanced at my mother, and Agent Edwards must have read the look that passed between us.

"I know what you're thinking, Cammie. The Circle has double agents, moles, traitors at every level of every agency. Well . . . that's why this task force doesn't report to *any* agency. We are very small. We are very select. We only have people we trust completely. And one of the people I trust most . . . is you. That is why I've come to ask a favor."

"I'm not doing any favors for you," I snapped.

"Hear him out, Cammie," Mom warned, but I raged on.

"Did you bring Preston here?" I asked, but I didn't really let myself be hopeful.

"No," Max Edwards said. "But there is something you and I need to discuss."

"Make no mistake about it, Agent Edwards, you can try to *make* me talk—you wouldn't be the first," I reminded him. "But that didn't work out so well the last time, so you can save yourself the trouble."

I started for the door.

"I'm not here to question you, Cammie." The man's words stopped me. "Not about Preston. Not about anything."

And I couldn't help myself. I turned and glared at him. "Then why *are* you here?"

He shrugged, as if looking for a way to finally say, "I guess because we need your help."

"I'm not helping you."

"It's not for me," he said, and I didn't move again. "As you know, when possible, we've been taking Circle members into custody. A few of the lower-level assets have been somewhat cooperative. But Mr. Winters . . . he is refusing to speak to anyone."

"What did you expect?" I laughed a little at his naïveté.

"I'm sorry." He smiled a condescending smile. "What I meant to say is that he refuses to speak to anyone . . . but you."

And at last I was surprised. For all of his experience and training, Agent Edwards and his task force needed me.

"As I told you earlier, Agent Edwards," Mom began, "my daughter does not have to go anywhere with you. She doesn't have to help you. She will not—"

"I'll do it."

"Cammie," my mother said, "you don't have to do this. You don't have to go and you do not have to help. It could be dangerous," she added, the last part a warning.

"That's true, Cammie," Agent Edwards said, walking toward me. "Your mother is right. So what do you say?"

"Yes," I told him. "I'll do it. I'll—"

But I never got to finish, because in the next second a syringe was in Agent Edwards's hand, and the needle was in my arm, and just that quickly my mother's office began to spin, the whole world spiraling quickly into black.

Chapter Thirteen

The room was black around me. A pounding, throbbing ache filled my head. I waited for my eyes to adjust to the darkness, but they didn't. Instead, I was swallowed by the hollow emptiness, uncertain how to break free.

I shivered and realized I was freezing cold. My uniform felt familiar against my skin, and I knew that no one had bothered to change my clothes in the time that I'd been unconscious. But how long had that been? A few hours? A few days? The last time I'd woken up in a strange place, I'd just lost months of my life, and that memory came pounding back then. My head hurt. My arms and legs ached. I felt something churning in my stomach, and I couldn't help myself, I was sick—vomit covered the floor, and I started to cry. I started to scream. I wanted out. I needed out. So I stood and pressed my hands against the walls.

I felt cold steel. Metal. Something man-made and foreign. And I knew that even though I was no longer being held by the Circle in Austria, I most certainly wasn't in the Gallagher Academy anymore, either.

Slowly, I eased down the wall, feeling my way as I went, forcing myself to breathe deeply, steadily.

"I'm okay," I said aloud to no one but myself. "I'm not lost. I'm not lost. I'm not—"

And then I found the lever. And then I turned it and felt the door shift against my hands. Light poured in, and I shut my eyes as I stumbled forward, out of the back of a van and into a massive, empty hangar. Bright fluorescent lights hung above; but inside there was nothing but the plain, unmarked van . . . and me.

"Hello, Cammie." I jerked my head upward and saw Max Edwards standing on the catwalk that ran across the top of the room. "Welcome back."

"Where are we?" I asked, my voice groggier than it should have been. My head pounded and swirled.

Agent Edwards was coming down the stairs, strolling easily toward me.

"I'm sorry you had to wake up alone like that, Cammie. I thought you'd sleep for at least another hour. Good thing I came to check on you."

I rubbed my aching head. "My grandma says I have a high metabolism. Besides, I'm really, really good at being knocked unconscious. I have a lot of experience with that."

Agent Edwards chuckled like he thought I was making a joke. I wasn't.

"You're not going to tell me where we are, are you?"

"No, Cammie. I'm not."

"Or *when* we are?"

"No again. A smart girl like you can use time to calculate distance, Cammie, and you know I can't let you do that. That wasn't part of the deal."

"Because this is need-to-know, and I don't?" I asked.

He smiled and shook his head. "Because you wouldn't believe me."

Max Edwards led the way down a long, narrow hallway. Cameras hung at regular intervals. It was all steel and concrete, and I felt the chill that seeped through the walls. "So how far underground are we?" I asked the man, who didn't say a thing.

We passed beneath a series of strange grates.

"Biohazard detectors?" I asked. "Air vents?"

Again, the man was silent, but I didn't need him to reply. I just needed him to take me to Preston, so I kept counting our steps, noticing the gradual incline of the hall. I wasn't exactly new to covert underground facilities, so wobbly head and upset stomach or not, I was starting to feel like I might be on slightly familiar ground. But then the hallway turned, and I came to an abrupt stop in front of the most intimidating door I'd ever seen.

"Well, this is special," I said while Edwards waved up at a security camera that was stationed overhead. "If I didn't know any better"—I talked on while Edwards placed his palm on a scanner and looked into a retinal image camera—"I'd say this is a door fit for a . . ."

The door sprang open, swinging wide, as I finished, ". . . *prison.*"

I glanced up at Agent Edwards, but again he said nothing. Still, I could see in his eyes that I was right.

There were guards and thick walls. Cameras covered every angle, not hidden, not disguised. It was a place built to remind you that Big Brother was watching.

The doors were made to lock down in a flash. It was all steel and chrome and concrete, and even if Edwards had had the forethought to pack me a jacket, I'm pretty sure I would have shivered.

"He shouldn't be in prison," I snapped at the man beside me. But Agent Edwards only laughed, a condescending huff that, despite the chill, burned me.

"Preston Winters is the next generation of one of the most powerful and notorious criminal families in the history of the world. Put your hand here, Cammie," he instructed, almost as an afterthought, but I did as I was told.

My palm stung, but I didn't let him see me wince.

Finally, the guards cleared us to go through yet another massive door. I felt Agent Edwards's hand on my back. If I hadn't known better, I would have sworn he was worried for me as he instructed, "Once in the room, Cammie, do not leave your chair. You cannot carry anything in your pockets or in your hair. Do not mention the day of the week or the time of day."

There, among those windowless rooms and artificial lights, I knew the game they were playing.

"I don't *know* the day of the week or the time of day," I reminded him.

"Of course." He didn't scold me. He sounded too nervous.

"This is wrong," I told him. "He doesn't deserve to be here."

"These are the rules, Cammie. Now, you can abide by them, or you can leave and we will have gone to a great deal of trouble for nothing. It's your call."

There comes a time in every spy's life when you don't have the luxury of caring. Emotion is a rarity, a commodity so precious that you have to dole it out in special, secret batches. Agent Edwards had passed that point. This was a place for people who had to be immune to what they did, to what it meant. And I didn't know if the chill inside the prison came from being underground or from the cold hearts of the people who filled it.

He looked at me as if I were still young and innocent, as if part of him envied me because I was still able to feel. A part of me wondered how much longer I had before my heart froze over too.

"Come, Cammie." He reached for the final door. "Your country needs you."

The first time I met Preston Winters he'd been twenty pounds too light for his frame, wearing clothes that were chosen by some focus group somewhere. He'd been too quick to smile—too easy to laugh. He'd been all about bad jokes and good eye contact, and I'd liked him. I'd liked him a lot.

But walking into the small, sterile room with a lone metal chair and a window of darkened glass, I couldn't imagine the boy I knew inside that place. The Preston Winters I'd met had been normal. Helpless. Free.

"I can stay with you, Cammie. . . ." Agent Edwards sounded nervous, afraid for me, as if part of him were starting to regret bringing me here and making me a part of this world. But it was *my* world too.

I thought about the scars on my body.

It was my fight.

So I turned to him. "Get out."

I walked nervously to the heavy metal chair in the center of the room and sat down, like I'd been told to do. In the reflection of the glass I could see the cameras trained on me. I had no illusion of privacy. Preston and I would be recorded from every angle; they wouldn't miss a single word. But at least I'd get to see him. At least I'd get to tell Macey he was okay.

I sat alone for ten minutes, but I didn't shift. I didn't waver. I wasn't about to let the men on the other side of those cameras see me sweat.

Then a buzzer sounded. The glass went bright, and I looked through to the other side at Ambassador Winters, who sat smiling back at me.

Chapter Fourteen

"Where's Preston?" I lunged forward and was almost off my chair before I remembered Agent Edwards's warning. I scooted back slightly but didn't dare let my gaze leave the ambassador's eyes.

"I don't know, Cammie," Winters told me. "You'd know better than I."

"I thought he . . ." I started before the truth finally settled down on me. "*You* wanted to see me?"

"Don't sound so surprised." The ambassador crossed his ankles. He looked perfectly at home there in a room exactly like mine. But he wore shackles around his hands and feet. "You're a very intelligent young lady. Maybe I missed your company."

"Don't be coy with me. And don't waste my time."

"Fine," he said.

"Why am I here?"

"I'm sorry about what happened, Cammie," he said, not answering my question.

"Sorry that you tried to have me killed, or sorry that I had enough dumb luck to avoid it?"

He shook his head—a *tsk, tsk, tsk* gesture that made my skin crawl. "You're very lucky, my dear. But you are anything but dumb."

"They said you wanted to talk to me—that I was the only person you *would* talk to. . . . So, what is it? What do you want to tell me?"

Despite the handcuffs and shackles, Winters leaned closer, looked into my eyes. "How are you, Cammie?"

He sounded like the man who had welcomed me into the embassy, embraced me like a friend. And I hated him for it. I hated him so, so much.

"No," I said. "You don't get to ask me that. You don't get to act like you're one of the good guys. Don't forget. Do not forget that *I know better*."

I watched the words sink in, and for a second I could have sworn a degree of sadness crossed his face. "I know you do, Cammie. But I'm still interested in your welfare."

I started to stand. "Good-bye, Mr. Winters. I wish I could stay and chat, but we've got this big test, and I'd really better be getting back to—"

"Wait, Cammie. Please."

"Tell me why you brought me here, or I go. Now. And I never come back."

"What do you know about the Circle, Cammie?"

He shifted then, not with his body but with his tone.

"Stop wasting my time," I told him again.

"I'm serious," he said. "Do you know when we were founded? By whom? *Why?*"

He put a special emphasis on the final word and that, at last, made me wonder.

"Cavan was a proud man," Winters went on. He didn't wait for me to answer. "He hated anyone who might have more power than he had."

"Get to the point," I snapped, and Winters talked on.

"Cavan wanted—no, *needed*—the Union to fail. A divided America was the only America he could stomach. And that meant he needed Lincoln to die. For the country to splinter, shatter. So the question is, Cammie, what does the Circle need *now?*"

For a second, I forgot he was a man who'd tried to kill me, and I looked at him like he was one of my teachers, like it was just another day back at school.

"The Circle wants power. They need profit."

"No, Cammie." Winters shook his head, but he didn't scold. "I'll admit, we allowed ourselves to stray from Cavan's original mission. We got greedy, hungry for physical wealth, and Cavan's original goal slipped from our minds. I do so admire the Gallagher Academy. It is still what *your* founder wanted it to be. Of course, Gillian Gallagher did it all without government involvement. I wonder what she would say if she saw the way the agencies have the run over your school today."

"You were a governor, an ambassador. You were almost president—and you mean to tell me that you hate the government?"

"Why should governments have more power than the people they're supposed to govern?"

"Is this supposed to be a social studies class? Because I haven't had one of those in ages."

"We strayed from our mission, Cammie. Zach's mother—Catherine—she's just one of our operatives who became greedy. But people like Catherine were only reflecting what they saw in our leadership. We lost sight of our ultimate goal, and now the Circle is crumbling. And so those of us in the Inner Circle decided that it is time to finish Cavan's original mission."

I thought back to Cambridge, the mad terror in Knight's eyes as he talked about whatever it was the Circle was planning. I had thought the truth had died with him, but there it was again—staring back at me through three inches of reinforced glass.

"What mission is it?" I asked, lurching forward. "What is the Inner Circle planning? Tell me how to stop it."

He leaned a little closer. The shackles on his wrists jangled as he pointed in my direction and said, "Elizabeth Sutton is a very smart girl."

The abrupt change in subject knocked the air out of me. I had wanted answers and I got games. "Don't talk about Liz," I snapped. "If that's some kind of threat—"

"I would never hurt Ms. Sutton. And you . . . well, you would do well to listen to her. She is wise beyond her years."

I shook my head and spat, "What does Liz have to do with this?" I was racked with confusion and fatigue. "Why am I here? Why are you telling me all of this? Why aren't you telling

them?" I pointed to the cameras that lined the room, covering every possible angle.

"Because I have a favor to ask of you, Cammie."

I watched his eyes grow darker. Any trace of happiness was gone. I no longer thought he was enjoying himself, playing with me. He was a desperate man. And he looked at me as if I were his only way out.

"What?" I snapped.

The ambassador looked down at his bound hands. "My son. He's not part of this, you know."

"Preston will be fine. He's in custody. Catherine can't get to him now."

The ambassador's eyes iced over. "None of us will ever be fine again. But my son can *help you stop it.*"

"What have they done?" I asked again, more urgent now. I thought about what Knight had told me. "The Circle leaders got together and put something into motion. What was it?" Impatience and fear were breaking through my voice. "Tell me what I have to do!"

He was opening his mouth to speak—the words were almost there. A few moments longer and Winters would have told me everything we needed to know, but they were moments we didn't have. Because before Preston's father could say another word, the glass that stood between us went black.

"Ambassador?" I yelled and glanced at the door, expecting a guard to knock—come in and tell me that my time was up. But no knock came. I looked at the cameras, but the tiny lights

were out and I knew that they were off. No one was watching. No guards were monitoring our conversation. I was alone in the quiet room, and I felt the hair on my arms stand on end. Everything was too still, too quiet, as I broke with protocol and rushed toward the glass.

"Ambassador! Ambassador, are you—"

I raised my hand and started to bang, but then I heard the sounds of a struggle on the other side. Sharp cracks filled the air—twice, in rapid succession, and I bolted away just as a third crack sounded.

The thick glass that separated the two rooms must have been bullet resistant—but not bulletproof—because the glass began to splinter, cracks spreading out like a spiderweb.

"Help!" I yelled into the cameras, but I knew no one would hear me.

I ran to the door and peered out the tiny window just in time to see the door to the next room open.

There was a small, basic lock on my door. It seemed out of place there in that high-security fortress; but I turned it anyway and backed away slowly, hoping that whoever had shot the ambassador wouldn't care about me. I was a visitor—a kid. There was nothing trapped inside of me that anybody wanted anymore. I was nothing, I told myself.

But then the doorknob moved.

Someone pushed, but the lock held; and I jerked backward just as something heavy crashed against the door.

In my head, lists were forming. Plans. Options. But the

fact remained that I was locked in a room with no weapons and no . . .

Window.

I picked up the metal chair and took aim at the center of the web that filled the heavy glass.

Out in the hall, someone banged against the door again, so I hit harder.

"Come on," I said to no one but myself. "Come—"

And then the glass shattered, falling to the floor. I jumped over the partition and into the other room, where the ambassador was still bound to his chair as he lay on the floor. Blood stained the concrete. His face looked almost peaceful as he stared up at me and gave me one last smile.

"Save Preston," he whispered, eyelids fluttering.

And then he died.

Chapter fifteen

Even as I watched the life drain out of Preston's father, I knew that I should run. And yet I felt like I should wait, hold his hand, tell him that his son was going to be okay. But there are some lies even spies can't tell a dying man.

The door to the room where I'd been sitting banged open, and I didn't wait for the shooter to realize I was gone—to see me on the other side of the shattered glass and follow. I leaped over the ambassador's lifeless body and hurled myself into the hall, running away from the interrogation rooms as quickly as I could.

But my breath came harder than it should have. I told myself that I'd eaten too much of Grandma Morgan's fudge over Christmas—that maybe the drugs they'd used to transport me there weren't entirely out of my system. Whatever the case, my legs didn't move as quickly as they should have. My breath was labored and heavy, and after a hundred feet, I wanted to double over and catch my breath, but I didn't dare slow down.

If I slowed down, I'd die.

I was deep underground in a facility so secure there were probably only a handful of people who knew it even existed, but someone from the Circle had found Winters there. Someone was still looking for me.

The corridor curved and branched, and footsteps echoed in the hallway. I looked for a way out, but then I realized a pair of guards was running toward me.

A deep voice ordered, "Spread out. *Find her.*"

I thought maybe I should trust them, but then I remembered I couldn't trust anybody.

So I pressed myself deeper into the shadows and the pair ran past. As soon as they were gone, alarms began to sound. The overhead fluorescents pulsed. The lights on the surveillance cameras began to blink, and I knew that the system was rebooting. It wasn't just a camera malfunction, the sirens said. The facility knew there was a breach, a gunman. A body. They would know that I was on the loose, and maybe they would blame me—how did I know? All I was sure of was that I wasn't safe there.

My side ached and my head hurt, and when the hallway branched, I stopped and looked and listened.

Heavy cables ran overhead, electrical lines that carried currents and pictures and sound. But one hall had fewer lines, so that was where I went.

I slowed my pace, moving carefully. There was a storage room that was locked. A vacant room that I thought must have been a cell. And then there was another door. Through the tiny window, I looked into what must have been a guardroom.

Monitors covered one wall, and on them I saw people walking in cells, sleeping on cots.

Red lights whirled. Gates swung shut. The images changed then, and I saw him.

"Preston."

He was asleep in a cell—I didn't know where. He looked so peaceful. So innocent. There was no way for him to know that somewhere in that labyrinth, his father's body was lying on the floor—that I still had his blood on my hands.

And then more than ever I knew I had to get out of there. I had to survive so that I could get him out too.

Thirty yards down the corridor, a metal barrier began to fall out of the ceiling, blocking off the only other exit. I had no idea what lay in that direction, but I knew I couldn't go back the way I'd come, so I bolted forward. My hands pumped at my sides. My lungs burned, but I didn't let that stop me as I dropped to the ground, sliding faster and faster. I felt the metal barrier graze against my hair—a few strands even caught in it—nothing but faint traces that I had been there as I made it to the other side.

There was an air shaft. I didn't know where it led or what would greet me on the other side, but what else was new?

Cold hit me as I opened the shaft.

I didn't think twice. I shimmied inside. And that was when I felt the fall.

You might think I'm exaggerating. But, believe me, this time I'm totally not. I felt myself begin to slide, with nothing to hold on to. No way to stop my descent. Suddenly, I burst free of the shaft and landed on what felt like a slab of solid ice.

But then even the ground gave way beneath me, and soon I was falling, tumbling. Snow covered me, and I rolled over and over. Freezing dampness clung to my hair and my skin. My teeth rattled, and instantly I understood why my breath had been so labored, why my head had hurt so much.

Agent Edwards hadn't brought me *down* to the facility. I clawed backward, easing across the ledge on which I lay.

He'd brought me *up*.

I looked out at a sky that was so blue it was almost too bright to look at. A few fluffy white clouds floated by. Ridges of mountains surrounded me, and everywhere there was snow and rocks and big pine trees heavy with needles.

Those weren't the Alps, I was certain. The air and the sky just felt different than they had last fall. My internal clock had reset itself somehow, and I knew the sun felt lower than it should have. I was north. Very, very north. Alaska, maybe? And I was alone, clinging to a narrow ridge, a foot from the edge of the world.

They'd come looking for me eventually, wouldn't they? Follow my tracks? Find me? But would they reach me before night fell and the temperature dropped? Never before had my uniform skirt felt so short, my sweater so thin. I couldn't stop shaking and telling myself that I had come too far to freeze to death on that mountain.

People would be looking for me. The gunman would get caught. I was going to be okay, but only if I kept going, so I didn't look back. A hundred yards down the steep face of the cliff, I saw a loading bay—what I assumed was probably the main entrance to the facility. So I set one foot in front of the other and got ready to make the climb.

Chapter Sixteen

THINGS TO EXPECT AFTER A SECURITY BREACH AT
MAYBE THE MOST SECURE PRISON ON THE PLANET
(ALSO, AFTER CLIMBING DOWN A MOUNTAIN):
(A list by Cameron Morgan)

- Hot chocolate. Seriously. The guards who find you
  are going to insist that you keep moving and change
  into warmer clothes, but the real medicine is hot
  chocolate. The hotter and the chocolatier the better.

- Turns out, if you escape from a high-level detention
  facility, really big, really macho guys stop looking
  at you like you're cute and start looking at you like
  you're awesome.

- After doing a climb like that with no gear and no
  help, nobody seems to think they need to drug you
  to get you OFF the mountain.

- The trip home takes A LOT longer when you're fully conscious.

- Long trips are an excellent time to think.

- You may totally not like what you're left to think about.

"Cammie!" Mom said as soon as I walked through the school's front doors. She rushed across the foyer and threw her arms around me. Then, just as quickly, she pushed me away—held me at arm's length—and examined me as if trying to make sure Agent Edwards was returning me in the same condition I'd been in when I'd left.

I wasn't. And my mother, spy that she is, could see so.

"Are you okay?" she asked, and I nodded.

"Yes. I'm fine."

But my mother just slid her gaze onto Agent Edwards. "Did they find out how the shooter got in?" she asked.

"Uh . . . yes." He spoke the word too carefully. "The gunman was a guard at the facility. He'd been turned."

"I see," Mom told him. "Kiddo." Mom smoothed my hair. Her hand cupped my face. "Why don't you go upstairs? Go to bed. You need your rest." Then Mom turned her full attention back to the man who'd brought me home. "I need to talk to Agent Edwards."

There was a feeling coursing between them—two veteran

operatives, powerful people, neither one used to backing down. I eased away, but I don't think Agent Edwards or my mother even noticed that I was still standing there. They were too busy staring daggers at each other.

"You have a lot of nerve bringing her back like this."

"Would you have rather she not come back at all?" the man asked.

"Don't be coy with me. She was supposed to be safe with you."

"I'm very sorry your daughter had to live through that," Agent Edwards said.

"*Live* being the key word, of course." Mom leveled a glare at him.

"What do you mean, Rachel?" Agent Edwards sounded tired and impatient and ever so slightly annoyed.

"I mean my daughter was flown to the far corner of this country only to see the ambassador killed and have the gunman turn on her."

"*Former* ambassador," Max Edwards corrected. "And as the head of the interagency task force, no one regrets his death more than I. He had information we needed, Rachel. After all, that's why your daughter was there."

Mom sidled closer. "And as soon as he started talking, he was killed? And the girl he was talking to was targeted?"

"It was regrettable."

Mom shook her head slowly. "To say the very least."

I watched my mother in that moment, the narrowing of her eyes, the straightening of her spine. She moved ever so slightly in front of me as if to block any more bullets that might be heading in my direction. And I knew what she didn't say: that I wasn't out of danger. Not by a long shot.

"It was an isolated incident," Edwards told her.

"Was it?" Mom asked. "Was it really? I thought your *task force* was impervious to moles."

"No one is taking this breach more seriously than I am, Rachel."

"Well, evidently you aren't taking it seriously enough," Mom said.

"What's that supposed to mean?"

"It means it's hard to sail a leaking ship," Mom told him. "Perhaps your mole-free, traitor-proof task force isn't quite as safe as you thought."

"Tell me, Rachel"—I watched the man shift, take a different tack—"where is Joe Solomon? Where is he right now?"

"Joe Solomon is dead." Mom's voice cracked. She'd spent enough time imagining what it would be like to lose him that it probably wasn't hard at all for her to pretend that she had. "He was killed in an explosion at the Blackthorne Institute last spring. As the head of the task force, I'm surprised you didn't know that."

"Of course." Edwards smiled. "How silly of me to forget." He stepped toward the door but glanced back at my mother. "I'm sure I'll be seeing you again soon." He nodded in my direction. "Cammie," he said, then opened the door.

He didn't turn back again, didn't falter. But even after he was gone, his presence lingered. I felt it in my bones, saw it in my mother's eyes as she kept her gaze trained on the front windows, watching the headlights of Max Edwards's car disappear.

"They know," Mom said. She didn't look at me. She just kept staring into the darkness, almost like she was waiting for black helicopters and SWAT teams to descend upon our grounds and swarm all over the mansion. "They know about Joe."

"They *suspect*," I tried to correct her; but Mom just shook her head.

"No, Cammie. They know. Or they think they know, and that is all they need."

"So what does that mean?"

"Joe's not safe here." Mom looked numbly at the closed door.

"The task force isn't going to work, is it?" I asked.

I waited for my mother to answer, but it was like I hadn't spoken at all. The answer was the silence that stretched between us.

"So what does that mean? Do we go back to looking for the Circle leaders ourselves? I think we've got to. We should call the Baxters, right? Maybe—"

"You should go to bed, Cammie."

At last, my mother looked at me, but it wasn't the look I'd grown used to. She didn't want to be alone. She looked at me like maybe it was the last time she'd ever see me—like that moment was precious and rare and fleeting. Only then did I realize just how close I'd come to never coming home again.

Mom hugged me and smoothed my hair. She kissed the top of my head, just like she'd done when I was a little girl.

"You're so grown-up, kiddo," she said, and I felt myself blush a little. "When did you get so grown-up? You don't even need me anymore."

"Of course I need you."

"No, Cammie." She held me tighter, looked into my eyes. "You've already handled situations that agents twice your age would crumble under. You're a tremendous operative. And you're ready, sweetheart. When the time comes, I promise you, you'll be ready."

"Okay," I said—because what else could I say? It was like my mother was talking in riddles, and I was far too exhausted to try to break the code.

"Now, go on. I'm sure it's killing Zach and the girls not to have all the details. Just promise me you'll try to get some sleep."

"I promise," I said.

"Cammie." Mom's voice stopped me. "I love you, sweetheart."

"I love you too," I told her, and then I walked away.

"So, Cammie," Bex's voice was cautious. It was a new approach for her, and it scared me. "How was it?"

"It was awful. They shot Ambassador Winters right in front of me. It was . . . awful," I said again. I didn't care how ridiculous I sounded.

"It's okay, Cam." Bex eased slowly closer. "Just tell us what you know."

"They knocked me out to take me there. I don't even remember leaving the mansion. And when I woke up I was groggy and sick. And then Agent Edwards realized I was awake and he took me inside the prison. I thought I was going to see Preston, but it was his dad instead. Preston's dad asked for *me*. And then they killed him. They shot Ambassador Winters. They shot him and then they came for me."

"Was Preston there?" Macey asked, but she didn't face me.

"He was in a cell in the facility. I didn't see him, though. I saw a video feed, and he was on it."

"Was he hurt?"

"He looked fine, Macey. Just fine. I didn't see him up close, but the ambassador was okay, so that tells me—"

"Until they killed him," Macey cut me off.

"What?"

"The ambassador was okay until they killed him—that's what you mean, right?"

"Don't think about this, Macey."

"Think about what? The truth? Because that is the truth, isn't it? Someone didn't want Winters talking, so they killed him. Because he knew something. And maybe Preston knows it too. Maybe now you know it. Maybe . . ."

"They'll come after me again?" I finished her thought in spite of how much I hated it. I didn't want to go back to being the girl the Circle of Cavan was chasing.

"What did Winters tell you, Cammie?" Bex was in front of me, staring into my eyes. If she could have reached into my head and pulled the truth out she would have, but all she could do was hold me perfectly still and say, "Think!"

"Cavan," I said. "We talked about the Inner Circle and Preston and . . ." I trailed off, stunned by what I remembered.

"What?" Macey asked.

"Liz," I whispered. "He talked about Liz."

"*This* Liz?" Bex asked, pointing in our roommate's direction.

"Yeah." I shook my head, the whole thing coming back in bits and pieces. "He asked about you." I looked at Liz, whose eyes were even bigger and bluer than usual. "He said how smart you are. It was almost like he was trying to tell me something."

"About Liz?" Macey asked. "That's ridiculous. I mean, no offense, you are smart. It's just . . ." Macey's voice trailed off as she turned to Liz, who had gone even paler. "I mean, it is ridiculous, isn't it?"

Liz's voice was so soft it trembled. "Maybe it's not."

Chapter Seventeen

Liz looked at all of us, blue eyes darting, filling with grief and fear and tears.

"Liz, you're scaring me," I finally said when her silence became too much.

"I think it's my fault," she blurted, and the tears silently rolled down her face. Her pale cheeks burned crimson, and the words came in ragged stops and starts.

"I think it was me."

"What's you?" Bex asked.

"Do you guys remember the tests? Before we started school?" Liz asked.

Bex shook her head. "There were no tests, Liz. We've been on break. Remember?"

"No. Not now. When we were sixth graders? Before we started here at all? There were those tests. Remember those?"

"Sure. We took a few tests," I said.

"Well, I took more," Liz said. "I took dozens. Hundreds.

Probably because my parents weren't spies. I don't know why. I just know that I was poked and prodded and questioned for months. Personality tests. IQ tests. Psych profiles."

"What about them, Lizzie?" Bex asked.

"The butterfly effect." Again, Liz's voice cracked. She brought her hands to her face.

"Sit down," I told her, but she didn't move. She just kept shaking her head back and forth, over and over, until I thought she might get dizzy.

"A butterfly flaps its wings over the ocean and there's a hurricane in Asia."

"We know what the butterfly effect is, Liz," Bex said, but it was like Liz never even heard her.

"All things are connected," Liz said. "Like dominoes. Like a house of cards. Like—"

"We're going to need more facts and fewer similes, Lizzie," I tried.

"It's all my fault!" she shouted again.

"Liz, am I going to have to hit you?" Bex asked. "Because I'm totally willing to hit you."

"I'm not hysterical, Rebecca." I don't know if it was the use of Bex's full name or the tone of Liz's voice but I knew right then that whatever Liz was worried about—it was real. And it was bad.

"Liz, calm down," I tried. "Breathe. What is your fault?"

"Think about it," Liz went on after a minute. "One of the tests I had to take was on abstract thinking. You know—big questions. Crazy theories. If the earth were in the path of a meteor made of cheese, how would you stop it? That kind of thing."

"Your tests had cheese meteor questions?" Bex asked. I shushed her, and Liz talked on.

"Well, one of the questions was 'How would you start World War Three?' That was it. A hypothetical. A crazy notion." Then her eyes got even bigger, her voice clearer. "I didn't know what I was doing. I didn't even know what the Gallagher Academy really was at the time. I just knew that it was really exclusive and I wanted to get in. I wanted to get in so badly. . . . So when they asked me how I'd start World War Three, I told them."

The idea washed around the room, settling on us all slowly, like someone had left a window open and the fog was rolling in.

"I thought it was just a hypothetical. It was supposed to *be a hypothetical*! But now . . ."

"What did you tell them?" I asked.

She looked up at me, absolute terror in her eyes. "I told them that World War Three would start with a tanker blowing up on the Iranian coast of the Caspian Sea and a bridge going out in Azerbaijan."

We'd talked about those tragedies at the Welcome Back Dinner, and I thought back to that night—how quiet Liz had been. How worried. And I realized how long Liz had been carrying that weight.

"Liz, I'm sure it's nothing," Macey said. "It was just a ship. It wasn't even a military ship. And that bridge was just—"

"A trade route," Liz cut her off. "More importantly, that bridge and the ports along the Caspian coast are *Iranian* trade routes. And with every route that gets cut off, the Iranians have to start using other routes that go through more and more volatile territories. Like Turkey or Afghanistan or Caspia."

Liz seemed exhausted, as if the sheer act of admitting it all out loud was about to be too much for her.

"I've been wondering about it for a while now. What if I was right? What are the odds of those things just randomly happening? And then . . . what if they *weren't* random?" Liz trembled, the last bit of color draining from her face. "Remember what Knight told you in Cambridge? That the Circle is planning something terrible and it has *already begun?*"

"Liz," I asked, "are you saying . . ."

"I think the Circle has my test. And I think they're using it to start World War Three."

Chapter eighteen

No one told Liz she was crazy. As far as I could tell, no one even thought it. Mainly because A) Liz's particular brand of crazy doesn't include being stupid. And B) Take it from the girl who spent most of the past semester being totally brainwashed—in our world, crazy never means impossible. And, besides, I didn't know what the Circle had done, but I did know they were capable of anything.

So we didn't panic as we ran downstairs. No one cried or yelled or sounded any alarms as we rushed through the dark and sleeping hallways. And yet there was a hurried, frantic pace to our steps—like this secret was on our heels and we had to outrun it.

My mother's office light was on and the door was closed.

"Mom," I yelled, banging on the door probably louder than I needed to. "Mom, it's me. I need to talk to you. It's an—"

But then the door opened, cutting me off.

"Ms. Sutton," Professor Buckingham said when she caught

sight of Liz. "What is wrong with you?" She eyed all four of us, with our untucked shirts and sloppy ponytails. We didn't look like trained covert operatives, I was sure. But I didn't care.

"We're looking for the headmistress," Macey said as if that were explanation enough. Professor Buckingham looked back as if it wasn't.

"She's not here, girls."

"She was *just* here," I countered.

Then I heard the voice. "Gallagher Girl?"

I turned and saw Zach in the corner of the office. His eyes were narrow and cautious.

Buckingham glanced in his direction, then explained, "I was just giving Zachary a message, and then I was going to come find you."

"We need to see the headmistress," Liz blurted, but Buckingham didn't waver.

"That was the message, I'm afraid," our teacher said. "Cameron, your mother and Mr. Solomon have been called away—"

"Called away?" Macey asked. "Where? When?"

"Just moments ago," Buckingham said, and I thought about the way my mom had hugged me in the foyer, the finality of her words, and, at last, I heard them for what they were. They weren't a good night. They were a good-bye.

"Something urgent has come up and the two of them had to . . . leave," Buckingham finished, choosing her words carefully.

"But—" Liz started, and Buckingham cut her off.

"But nothing. Listen to me very carefully, girls. They had to go. They will be gone indefinitely, and they will be unreachable. Do not try to follow them," Buckingham warned. "Do not try to track them down. If you want them to be safe then you will follow these instructions. Do you understand?"

I did understand, but that didn't mean I had to like it. I looked at Liz and thought about what our oldest faculty member was really telling us: that the people we trusted most were gone. And there was no way to know when—or if—they would ever return.

Buckingham started through the Hall of History.

"Your mother is fine, Cameron. She will be back soon." She looked certain. She sounded sure. But she held my gaze just a moment too long. Her hands shook, and in that moment, Patricia Buckingham didn't look like a seasoned operative. She looked like an old woman, and it was harder than it should have been to watch her walk away.

"You need a coat," Zach told me an hour later. Then he took off his own jacket and slipped it around my shoulders. Because even major security threats of global proportions couldn't stop my boyfriend from being pretty much the sexiest guy alive.

We were standing in the space I'd first found a year before. Once upon a time it had been home to the Gallagher Academy's covert carrier pigeon program. Then Mr. Solomon had used it to decipher my father's final words to me. And now it was my favorite place to hide. With a small balcony and a secluded cave-like room, I felt free there, looking out over the school grounds and the lights of distant towns.

"I don't get it." Liz shook and paced. "Why would they leave? They can't just leave!"

"Cam," Bex said, inching closer. "You don't seem surprised."

"I'm not." I laughed at my own foolishness. "It was Edwards," I said. "When he brought me home, he asked about Mr. Solomon—like he knew he was still alive and hiding out here . . . like Edwards and his task force were going to come after Mr. Solomon and anyone who might be helping him."

I felt like an idiot that I hadn't seen what Mom was saying in that moment. I speak fourteen different languages. I should know "good-bye" when I hear it.

"So now they're just gone?" Macey asked.

"They're on a mission, Macey," Zach reminded her. "If what happened at the prison proves anything, it's that nothing has changed. The Circle has moles everywhere. Even within Max Edwards's little task force. If we want to stop the Circle's leaders, then we are going to have to track them down ourselves." Zach crossed his arms and leaned against the balcony's railing. "That's what Rachel and Joe are going to do."

He was right, and I wanted to say so. But a thought I couldn't articulate had settled in my mind, and I felt myself turning it over and over like a talisman.

"What is it, Gallagher Girl?" Zach asked.

I shook my head. "I don't know. It's just . . . something isn't right."

Technically, a whole lot of *somethings* weren't right, but there was one I couldn't put my finger on, and that, more than anything, haunted me. I wanted to ask my mother for advice. I needed to talk to Abby. I wanted Joe Solomon to fly in like the pigeons and start asking me questions until I landed upon the answer my mind knew but couldn't say. I had been on my own for months last summer. But I'd never felt more alone in my life.

"What do we do now?" Liz asked. "Who do we tell about my test and . . . you know . . . World War Three?"

It sounded so silly when she put it that way—so crazy and far-fetched; but Liz was the smartest person I knew, and Liz wasn't just serious. She was terrified.

"Liz, are you sure you're right about this?" I asked. "Are you telling me that five and a half years ago you said that a person would have to do these exact things to start World War Three?"

"Well . . ." Liz looked slightly guilty. "Not these things exactly."

Bex opened her mouth to protest; but, for once, Liz was too fast for her.

"I said it would be about oil and the trade routes of the Gulf. I said that to escalate the tension in the region, one would need to eliminate the trade options for Iran and drive over eighty percent of their oil traffic through the pipelines they have going through Caspia."

"Caspia is a police state," Bex said.

"Exactly. There was a coup d'état fifteen years ago, and a bunch of military higher-ups took over the government and got rid of the royal family. King Najeeb has been living in exile ever since. The royal family had close ties to the West and an alliance with Turkey. But the military dictatorship that now rules Caspia is loyal to Iran. The whole thing almost blew up ten years ago, but that led to—"

"The Treaty of Caspia," I said. "Mr. Smith talked about that for a solid week our eighth grade year."

"Exactly," Liz said. "Caspia is a no-man's-land. Neither Iran nor Turkey can officially cross the border. But if more and more of the Iranian oil traffic has to go through there, then that border starts looking more and more tempting to the Iranian forces." Then Liz shrugged. "At least that was my theory."

"What does that mean, Liz?" Bex asked with a shake of her head.

"It's not science, okay? It's a butterfly—"

"Effect, we know," Bex finished for her.

"No! You don't know. I'm telling you that someone has my essay."

"And that's why we can't tell anyone, Lizzie," I explained. "If you gave that answer to the Gallagher Academy, then that means the Circle got it from the Gallagher Academy. We have no idea who we can trust." I took a deep breath. "Besides, it's not like these things are covert. Everyone in the world knows what's going on."

"So?" Liz asked.

"So are you *sure*, Liz?" Bex finished. "I mean, it sounds like the best spies in the world think these things are unrelated. Flukes."

"And things are never more than they appear?" The

question cut us to our core. "Besides," Liz added, "I think the best spies in the world are right here. And I'm asking them to believe me."

"Can you get a message to Mr. Solomon?" I asked Zach, who shrugged.

"Maybe. There's a dead drop I can use, but there's no way of knowing when he'll get the message. Or *if* he'll get the message."

"What about your mom?" Macey asked me.

"The same. We have to assume every means of communication in and out of the school is being monitored."

"So what does that mean, really?" Liz asked me.

"I guess . . . I guess it means we're on our own."

Chapter nineteen

THINGS THAT TOTALLY FREAKED ME
OUT IN THE DAYS THAT FOLLOWED:
(A list by Cameron Morgan)

- My mom and Mr. Solomon. I had no idea where they were or what they were doing. When—or if—they'd return. You may think spies would be used to that feeling, but spy kids? We never do get over it.

- Liz. It was the only time I'd ever seen her depressed about getting a test answer *right*.

- There was currently a non-zero chance that the Circle of Cavan wanted me dead. Again.

- Having people want me dead was something I was actually starting to get used to.

———

"Hello, girls. Welcome back," Madame Dabney said as we walked into Culture and Assimilation class the next morning. She walked down the row of tables that served as desks. There were lace tablecloths and silver candles. It always felt like we were going to tea, and in that room we sat straighter than any-place else on earth. In that room, we were ladies.

She handed us each a stack of papers.

"What you have here is our best idea of what your gradu-ation and placement examinations will contain. The written test, of course. Your practical exams . . . well, they could be anything. And make no mistake, they could come at any time."

I thought about all I'd seen and done. My life had been a test for years.

"On the twenty-eighth we will be taking senior portraits."

Madame Dabney handed the packets to the first girl in each row and we took turns taking one and handing the rest to the girl behind us.

"Those of you wishing to schedule summer internships must return these applications to my office by the fifteenth of next month," Madame Dabney said, sending along another stack of forms.

"Letters of reference for placement in any of the US agen-cies are required no later than April first. Please do not wait until the last minute to request these, ladies," Dabney warned. "That, more than anything, can ensure you receive a bad one."

Finally Madame Dabney walked back to her desk. "And, of course," she said, "the annual career fair is tonight."

"Tonight?" I blurted, totally not realizing I was speaking aloud.

"Yes, Cameron. Due to the . . . events . . . of last fall we decided to host the career fair in the spring semester this year." She passed another piece of paper down the long rows. "Here are the agencies and programs that will be attending. And do remember, ladies, this is not just their opportunity to get to know you. It is your chance to get to know *them*." She smiled. "You're seniors. Take this opportunity very, very seriously. Your futures will be here soon."

I looked down at the piles of paper that lay on the lace cloth before me. I'd been running for days. I'd been hiding for years. But Madame Dabney was right. My future was on my tail, and there was no way I could lose it.

Chapter twenty

That night, the Grand Hall didn't look like the Grand Hall. All the tables were gone, pushed to the sides or moved to another room. Booths lined the walls. I walked up and down the aisles. Alcohol, Tobacco, Firearms, and Explosives had set up a mock firing range where the teachers usually sat. There were MI6 and Interpol. The FBI and CIA.

"Hi," one clean-cut man said, pushing a brochure in my direction. "Have you considered a career with Homeland Security? We are the agency of the future."

"The US State Department," a woman said as I passed. "The world is our office."

There were seventh graders, loading up on Tootsie Rolls and free erasers from the US Marshals Service (they make people disappear). To tell you the truth, I'd seen it all before. I'd heard all the pitches, read all the material. The years changed; the booths grew. But I didn't have any better idea of what my future was going to look like.

"Hello," a man in an FBI polo shirt said, "do you know where you're going to be a year from now?"

I looked him in the eye. "That is an excellent question."

Truthfully, I would have been happy just knowing where my mother and Mr. Solomon were *right then*.

"Official FBI Post-it pad for your thoughts." I turned to see Bex behind me, holding out a bag full of loot. Part of me wanted to smile, but I couldn't. I just looked around the big room I knew so well and wondered why everything felt so utterly unfamiliar.

"I don't like this," I said.

Bex, being excellent at both spying and best-friending, didn't ask me what I meant. She just slid her arm through mine and told me, "They're out there, Cam. And they're okay. And they'll be back whenever it is best for them to come back and not a minute before."

"I know," I said, and then it was like the crowd parted. I could see Liz staring up at a huge display from the National Security Agency, offering prizes to anyone who could crack the codes they had on their walls.

"So, do you have it?" the recruiter asked her, but Liz shook her head.

"I don't know," she said and turned away.

"I don't like *that*," I said, and Bex nodded in grave agreement.

"Hey, Lizzie," Bex said when we reached her.

When I put my arm around her shoulders, I realized they were even thinner than usual. She was pale as a ghost except for the dark circles that ringed her eyes. Guilt weighed on her, and I for one was terrified of how far it might drag her down.

"Let's get out of here," I told her. "What do you say? Movies in the common room? We can go down to the labs, use liquid nitrogen to make ice cream. You know how that always cheers you up."

But Liz just stared blankly ahead. "I'm not hungry."

When I followed her gaze I saw what she was staring at. Interpol had brought a map of the world, and it hung on the wall by their booth. It looked so small, not even as wide as two of our regular dining tables. It looked so big, filled with tiny towns and vast wildernesses. Every good operative knows that the world is small, but the planet is big. No one knew where my mom and Mr. Solomon were. No one knew where the Circle would strike next.

Except someone *did* know.

I looked at Liz again. "It's okay," I told her.

"Is it?" Liz isn't one for snapping, but something in her tone froze me, shamed me. Made me feel small and helpless and weak.

"Liz, it's going to be okay. I—"

"Hello, Cammie." Agent Edwards was there, walking from the Interpol booth. Closer to me.

I shouldn't have been surprised to see him. We'd first met at the career fair my sophomore year—when I was still sneaking off to see Josh. History, after all, always repeats itself.

"How are you doing?" he asked.

"Fine," I said and tried to walk away.

"I hope this means you're considering a future with Interpol.

I told you a long time ago that we would love to have you. I meant it then. I still do."

"Thanks," I managed to mutter.

"We'd have room for your friends, too."

This made me stop.

"Ms. Baxter and Ms. McHenry—they are interested in fieldwork, are they not? And I think everyone in this room would love to work with Ms. Sutton."

When he talked about my friends, it didn't sound like an offer. It sounded like a threat.

"I'm sorry, Agent Edwards. My friend isn't feeling well. We've got to—"

But then he stepped closer, blocking me off from Bex and Liz, who had already started moving away.

"I was hoping to speak to your mother. Is she here?" Something in the way he spoke told me that he was measuring his words carefully. He didn't want to push me too far, too fast. But that didn't mean he didn't want to push me.

I didn't answer, and my silence made Max Edwards laugh. "I guess not. You know, I've been thinking. Funny thing about what happened with Winters, Cammie."

"I didn't think it was very funny," I told him, but Edwards talked on as if I hadn't spoken at all.

"The gunman disabled the security cameras, did you know that?"

"Yes."

"So we don't know what the two of you discussed." He

eased slightly closer. It was supposed to intimidate me, rattle me, make me want to talk. But it didn't. It made me want to fight. "What did Samuel Winters tell you?"

"You debriefed me the day it happened, remember? I already told you everything I know."

"Tell me again. *What did you and Winters talk about?*"

I cocked my hip and stared up at him. "Traitors. The weather. All the usual stuff."

"There's something I have to wonder, Cammie. Did the gunman turn on you because of what you heard?"

"To tell you the truth, I've gotten kind of used to the Circle of Cavan trying to kill me. I don't really stop and ask questions anymore."

But that wasn't true. I *did* ask questions. All the time. And I almost never liked the answers.

"Tell me, Cammie . . ." He tilted his head, studying me like I was an abstract piece of art; like he wasn't exactly sure what to see in me. "What else are you hiding?"

I should have listened to the inflection in his words—heard the tiny voice inside of me that said something was a little off about the question. But we were inside the Gallagher Academy. These were people who were in on the secret, aware of the truth. I was behind our walls. I was safe.

Or so I thought.

"Where is Joe Solomon?" He looked around, as if trying to see all my usual hiding places, peek through the cracks in the mortar.

"He's—" I started, but Agent Edwards cut me off.

"Don't say he's dead, Cammie. Do not lie to me." Then Max Edwards held out his cell phone; on it I saw an image of Mr. Solomon walking through a busy train station. He wore a ball cap and sunglasses, but there was no mistaking the man in the picture.

"That was taken this morning in London."

"Then why are you asking me where he is?" I said, but Edwards only smiled in response.

With a finger he swiped at the screen, and the image changed. I saw the area just to Mr. Solomon's right in the photo. I saw that he was holding my mother's hand.

A cold feeling filled my chest, and I knew what he was saying—what the photo meant. My mother and my teacher weren't coming back anytime soon. My mother would be on the run maybe for the rest of her life.

"So there you have it. You know Mr. Solomon isn't in the mansion. I guess you'll have to be leaving now."

"Oh, Cammie. You know better than anyone that Joe Solomon isn't the only Gallagher Academy resident who has spent time inside the Circle."

The ice that had filled my chest just moments before began to crack. It was like my whole world was shattering, and even though I hadn't seen Zach enter, some part of me knew what I would see as soon as I turned. He was standing by the Homeland Security booth. He was searching the crowd, looking for me. He was just another teenager thinking about the future until I shouted, "Zach! Run!"

* * *

Maybe it was instinct. Maybe it was training. But Zach wasn't like the stupid people you see in the movies. He didn't ask what I was shouting about. He didn't have to be told twice. In a flash, he was bolting down the aisle, running toward the foyer.

"Stop!" one of the recruiters yelled from the far side of the Grand Hall. He lunged at Zach, but the angle was wrong and Zach easily pushed him aside and kept on powering toward the door. Agent Edwards must have positioned someone there because soon a woman was lunging in front of Zach, trying to knock him off his feet. He dove, sliding beneath her, across the hardwood floor and into the foyer. And when the woman turned to follow, Bex was there.

"No," Bex said simply, a warning. Something in her voice stopped the more senior operative cold. Besides, Zach was already gone.

"Follow him!" Agent Edwards yelled just as I started to jerk away—to go rushing after Zach—but Agent Edwards had an iron grip on my arm. "No, Cammie. Stay," he ordered.

I pulled my free arm back, ready to punch and kick and claw my way out of there if I had to, but then a familiar voice stopped me in my tracks.

"Agent Edwards," Buckingham snapped, "what is the meaning of this?"

"Stay out of it, Patricia." The man tightened his grip on my arm and spun on the Gallagher Academy's oldest faculty member. But she's not our weakest. Not by a long shot.

"You are a guest in these halls," Buckingham said. The

words were tinged with anger and disappointment, and her accent wasn't genteel just then. It was frigid. "Now, let go of her."

"We are authorized to bring in *anyone* who has information about the Circle of Cavan."

"You don't have authorization from *me*!" Buckingham said.

Agent Edwards released my arm and pushed me toward two of the goons who had come with him. "I assure you, Patricia, we have no desire to harm the girl."

"That girl is a student of this school and under its protection."

"This school . . ." He huffed. "*This school* has been hiding and protecting Joe Solomon for over a year!" I was inching back, farther away from the man and his fury. "*This school* took in a known child of the Circle and then allowed four of its students to attempt to save another!"

Madame Dabney came running forward. "Patricia, what's the meaning of this?"

But Professor Buckingham never took her gaze off Agent Edwards. "These men were just leaving."

"Oh, we'll leave." Agent Edwards laughed. "But we won't be leaving alone."

"Cammie!" Professor Buckingham shouted. "Now!"

Chapter twenty-one

I didn't have to be told twice. I'd been given a direct order from a teacher. I knew what I had to do. I could hear the commotion behind me. Buckingham took a globe from the CIA's booth and hurled it at Agent Edwards's head, and when he ducked she brought a knee up into his face, bloodying his nose and knocking him, disoriented, to the ground.

Madame Dabney tripped one of the two goons who were supposed to be capturing me and pushed the other into the Secret Service's booth, sending a perfectly scaled replica of the White House crashing to the floor.

In a flash, the entire Grand Hall was in chaos. It was like a street fight. A brawl.

Seventh graders jumped onto the backs of FBI agents. Seniors squared off against the CIA. It wasn't cat versus mouse; it was spy versus spy, and I didn't turn around to look at the destruction that I was leaving in my wake.

I was too busy trying to think: Where would Zach go?

What would Zach do? He had to get away from the people chasing him, lose them somewhere in the classrooms or halls. Or passageways.

Hiding would have been easy—he had home-court advantage. But hiding wasn't going to be enough. If they knew he was at the Gallagher Academy, he wasn't going to be safe at the Gallagher Academy. Zach was going to have to run.

And then I knew where he'd be going.

I grabbed the banister of the nearest staircase and flung myself around, taking the steps two at a time, desperate not to be followed. And then I darted down the narrow hall lined with larger, more private rooms until I reached the only one that wasn't used by a teacher.

When I reached the door of Zach's room I burst through without knocking, which—to tell you the truth—was something of a mistake, because before my eyes even adjusted to the black, I felt a blow knocking me forward, off my feet and into the dresser.

"Gallagher Girl," Zach said. He sounded furious and ashamed, both.

"Are you okay?" His hands were on me then, checking my head and my arms.

"I'm fine."

"I'm so sorry. I thought you were—"

"I know."

"Who are they?" he asked.

"Interpol. CIA. They're everyone, Zach. And they're looking for you."

There was a backpack on his bed. He never carried it to class, and immediately I knew that it wasn't for textbooks and homework. He kept that bag packed and ready at all times, just in case he had to run.

I knew because I had a bag just like it.

I heard noises, footsteps pounding up the stairs.

"Come on," I said, reaching for his hand. "We've got to disappear."

And then I led him down the hall. When we reached a maintenance closet, I pulled him inside. It was too small, though. I'd never shared it with anyone before, and I found myself pressed against Zach, his arms around me, his backpack at our feet.

"That's his room!" someone said. They knocked down the door of his bedroom while Zach and I stayed pressed together in the black. "Find them!"

"Are you going to hide me in here forever?" he whispered.

"Maybe," I whispered back.

"He's been here," the men outside said. "He's gone."

"Or maybe"—I ran my hand up Zach's chest, put my arms around his neck—"I am just going to do this."

And then I pulled the lever. I watched Zach's eyes go wide as the floor beneath us gave way and together we dropped straight down, sliding through the ventilation system of the school, shooting like a dart away from the people trying to find us.

* * *

"You're crazy," Zach said when we finally landed with a thud two floors down.

"I'm a good person to know, Zachary. You should have figured that out by now."

"Oh . . . I have."

"Okay, lovebirds," said a voice behind us. I turned to see Bex, Liz, and Macey standing watching us, arms crossed. "Let's go."

It wasn't the time to tease. It wasn't the place to flirt. So I led the way through the inner workings of the school. We didn't speak again. Not when we stood pressed together and listened through a vent to two FBI agents discussing Zach's whereabouts. No one asked for an explanation when I found a length of rope and used it to lower myself into the basement level.

I thought back to a dark street in D.C. *Get her.*

I heard the shots in the prison and the yells of the guards. *Find her.*

I felt the people at my back. *Find them.*

And in my heart I knew that the girl I'd been on New Year's Eve was foolish. It wasn't yet time for me to stop running.

"This is it," I said when we pushed out of the basement and into a small shack that sat near the edge of the trees. "Over there," I said, pointing to a section of the main fence covered with overgrown rosebushes and thorns. "There's another tunnel there. It will lead us to town."

"Okay." Zach took a deep breath and turned to me. "I guess this is good-bye. For now."

"I'm going with you," I said.

The words hit Zach, and he looked between me and my friends, already knowing what would come next.

"And where she goes, we go." Liz folded her thin arms across her chest.

"Cammie, your mom's going to come back," Zach told me, and I couldn't help myself—I turned and looked back at the school.

Lights burned in every window. A searchlight swept across the grounds. I heard barking dogs and shouting men. The search would widen and spread, and it wouldn't stop until it found Zach.

Found *us*.

"No." I shook my head. "They're gone. And they can't ever come back."

"Gallagher Girl," Zach started, but I cut him off with a nod.

"*Them.*" The word was a whisper. "He said *find them.* That's why it isn't safe for me to stay." I reached up and gripped his shirt, made him face me as I said, "Think about it, Zach. Winters, Preston, you . . . They're coming for anyone who has ever been inside the Circle."

"Which is why it isn't safe for you to come *with* me."

"But I *was* inside the Circle—all last summer. Winters would only talk to me." I watched Zach shake his head, try to cast aside the thought he didn't want to dwell on. "I'm going," I said.

"*We're* going," Bex corrected.

"Fortunately," Macey added with a smile, "I had the fore-sight to pack Liz's van with various essentials."

Liz blushed. "I might have helped."

"No," I said.

"But . . . I brought gummy bears," Liz said as if that should be enough to neutralize any potential problem.

"If you leave now, you won't get to come back. Go to class." I looked at Liz. "Graduate. Leave, and we don't know what will happen. Which is why the three of you should stay."

"You really think we're going to do that?" Macey sounded like she might laugh.

"I think the three of you have never run away before." I looked down at the ground, the only memory I had of last sum-mer flashing through my mind.

"Leaving can't be nearly as hard as being left, Cam," Bex warned. Something in her voice said she still hadn't forgiven me—that maybe she never would.

I looked at our stone walls and iron fences, and even though we were perfectly dry, I had to shiver a little, thinking about Rome, about when my friends and I had been stuck on opposite sides of the river, no safe way to cross. I felt like my sisterhood and I were about to be on different sides of a vast expanse. I'd have to keep swerving, dodging, running, hoping someday to meet again.

"If we're going, we have to go now," Macey said.

And with that it was decided. We couldn't stay at school forever. After all, we'd spent years preparing for life beyond its walls. We just never knew we'd be rushing out to meet it quite that quickly.

"This way," I said, pulling back the branches of a rose-bush that, rumor said, had been planted by Gilly herself during the Civil War. Behind it was one of the oldest passageways at our school. It dated back to the Underground Railroad, and I knew we weren't the first desperate people to find it, to need it, to enter into darkness hoping to find a little light at the tunnel's end.

Zach went first. Then Bex and Macey and Liz. I was supposed to bring up the rear, yet I stopped for a moment, took one last look at the gray stone building, the lacrosse field, and the frost-covered line of trees. In the moonlight it looked almost like a painting. Like a dream. And maybe it had been that for me once. But now, whether I liked it or not, it was time to wake up.

"Cammie!" someone called through the dark. I turned to see Professor Buckingham standing at the door. She was looking at me. Her hair was a mess and her dress was ripped.

Part of me thought that I was in trouble, grounded, facing detention for life. But then Buckingham smiled and raised her hand in something that wasn't quite a wave, not quite a salute. It was more like she was reaching up to grab a fistful of that night air, to hold it like a memory.

"Good luck," she yelled, then turned and hit a button on the wall.

Instantly, the sirens began to screech. "Code Black. Code Black. Code Black."

Lights swirled. Titanium shutters covered all the windows. Barriers slid into place over every door, blocking me off from my teachers, my school. My home. Locking the men and women who'd been sent to find me inside one of the most secure buildings on the face of the earth.

There was only one way left to go, so I turned and started down the dark and dusty tunnel. And for the second time in my life, I ran away.

Chapter Twenty-two

I've never been a fugitive before.

I've been a runaway, a chameleon, an amnesiac. A spy. But fugitive was new to me, though I have to admit, not entirely unexpected.

We took shifts, driving down two-lane blacktop and interstates, winding mountain roads. We backtracked and sidetracked and did every countersurveillance thing any of us had ever learned. But, most of all, we drove. Not stopping, not resting through the night.

"We're here."

I heard Macey's voice and felt the van come to a stop, bolting upright despite the weight of Liz sleeping across me.

"Ten more minutes," Liz mumbled. Part of me wanted to let her go back to sleep. Part of me wanted any excuse I might have to think the night before had been a dream.

"Uh, Macey," Bex asked, straightening. She scooted up to lean between the front seats. "Where exactly is *here?*"

And then I saw what Bex was seeing. Miles of white-sand beaches stretched out on either side of us. The van sat in the center of a circular driveway. There were intricate iron gates and a massive fountain that was dry and full of leaves. The sky was gray, just like the ocean, and as soon as Macey opened her door I heard the waves crashing into land.

But all of that paled in comparison to the house. (And when I say "house" what I really mean is "mansion.") It was at least three stories tall with balconies and shaker shingles, and something about that moment made me feel like I'd fallen asleep in an old Dodge minivan and woken up in another world. In Macey's world.

"Come on," Macey said.

"Macey . . ." Bex sounded cautious. "We probably shouldn't stop."

"Well, I'm stopping," Macey said, spinning on us. "And I'm eating a real meal and finding a real bed. So . . . we can rough it. Or we can *rough* it." She pointed at the mansion. "And I, for one, need a shower."

She was out of the van and starting toward the doors. Bex and I began to run after her, but Zach was already there.

I don't think he'd slept. I didn't remember him eating. He looked exactly how he'd looked the moment we left the school. Alert and alive and more than a little like a cross between Joe Solomon and Agent Townsend.

"We have to stay off the grid, Macey. It's not safe for us to go anywhere anyone might think to look for us."

"Relax." She tried—and failed—to push past him. "It

belongs to some friends of my parents. They're in the middle of a really nasty divorce and the judge has barred both of them from the premises. The housekeeper isn't even allowed in, so trust me. We have the place to ourselves."

"We can't just break into a house, Macey," Liz said.

But Macey only smiled and reached into a potted plant by the front door. Moments later, a key dangled from her fingers. "Who said anything about breaking?"

Creeping inside the big, empty house, I had to admit that Macey was right. No one had been there for ages. I looked around the shadowy rooms. Heavy curtains hung over all the windows. Sheets covered the furniture. The refrigerator was empty, but the pantry was stocked, and so we ate soup and crackers and kept the curtains drawn and the lights off.

We slept all day and paced all night, and even the moon felt like a searchlight, sweeping across the ocean.

"Well, I'll say this for Macey," Zach whispered as he walked up behind me, "I like her idea of roughing it."

I was sitting in an Adirondack chair on the deserted stretch of beach, looking out at the ocean. I'd pulled the world's softest blanket off one of the guest beds and was sitting in the dark with it wrapped around my shoulders, my feet buried in the sand.

"We have five grand in cash and ten fake IDs," I said to Zach. I didn't turn to face him. The facts just came pouring out of me, unstoppable. "We have six credit cards, but I don't trust two of them. They can be traced back to the school, so . . . We'll need to get the van off the road. Too many people know it. We've used it too many times. So that leaves buses, I guess. We'll have to—"

"Cammie." My name was a whisper on Zach's lips, and he eased closer.

"The girls did a good job packing." I didn't think about when they'd done it—how they'd known. But every spy knows that running away is always a possibility. "We have basic comms and Liz has enough computers to hack NASA. We still need physical gear, though. Sporting goods. Electronics. We'll need a hardware store at some point. We should split up for that part."

"Cam." Zach kneeled in the sand in front of me. He took my hands. I hadn't realized how cold they were until he rubbed them in his own. "We need to talk about them."

"What about them?"

"Is this what's best for them?"

"We're going to need a team, Zach. We're going to need *this* team."

"We don't need a team to run, Gallagher Girl. I can't go back because my mom is part of the Circle. You're in danger because of what the ambassador may or may not have told you. *We've* got to go to ground. You and me. We have to run. Hide. *Disappear.*" He said the last word more slowly. I knew how big it was and what it meant. "And it will be easier if it's just the two of us."

"I'm not going to ground, Zach." I'd been thinking it for hours, weighing it. Worrying about it. So I stood and started toward the house. It was like all roads had been leading to that sandy beach for ages. Since I woke up in the Alps. Since I fell down a laundry chute in Boston. Since I pulled a pop bottle out of a trash can and said hello to a boy who had seen me in a crowd.

"Where are you going?"

I looked at the first boy who had ever seen me—the real me—and I told him, "To end it."

"We need to talk," I said as soon as I stepped inside.

"Good. You're here. We need to figure out a way to make contact with your mom." Bex was pacing. "My mum will know how. We just have to—"

"No." I shook my head and read her eyes. "Bex, what is rule number seven for an operative in deep cover?"

Bex knew the answer, but she didn't say it.

"An operative in deep cover operates alone without risking the safety and security of others," I said, rattling off one of the many things I'd learned from Joe Solomon. "There are maybe a half dozen people on this planet we can trust, and if you think they aren't going to be under constant surveillance, you're crazy. Which means"—I took a deep breath—"from this point forward, we're on our own."

"But . . ." The words seemed hard for Liz; the weight of all that was happening was far too heavy for her small shoulders. "We have to tell someone. About my test, about what the Circle is doing. Someone has to do something about it!"

"Someone *is* going to do something about it, Liz." I looked around the group. "*We're* going to do something about it."

"Cam, let's think about this," Zach told me, and I spun on him.

"I was supposed to sleep longer!" I heard myself shouting.

As random outbursts go, that was a pretty good one. I watched my roommates look at each other—at Zach. I watched them try to see what I was saying, so I talked on.

"Something has been bothering me ever since Preston's dad died. The drugs they used to knock me out on the way to the prison . . . they wore off too soon. Our theory has always been that the Circle sent a gunman to kill the ambassador *before* he could talk to me. Silence him. I wasn't even supposed to *be* with the ambassador when the gunman came. That was the story, right?"

"We know, Cam," Bex told me.

I shook my head. "But what if it was just a story? What if I was exactly where I was supposed to be—exactly when I was supposed to be there?"

I watched the people I know best look at me like I was a crazy person. Trust me. It's a look I know pretty well.

"Remember what you told me in London, Bex? That the Circle doesn't need me dead anymore because it's too late to stop me from telling anyone about the list?"

"Yeah, Cam," Bex said.

"You said that they didn't *need* me dead, but they'd probably still try to kill me if it was convenient—just for spite. Remember that?"

"Yeah, but—"

"Well, what if it was convenient? What if someone wanted me in that room? What if someone meant for me to die too?"

"Someone like Max Edwards?" Zach asked.

I nodded. "If I was supposed to sleep for another hour, why did he come check on me when he did? Why take me in to see the ambassador early? I mean . . . maybe it was all a coincidence. . . ."

"Or maybe it wasn't," Bex said.

"The Circle has moles everywhere," Liz said. "Even on his task force."

"Maybe they have one leading the task force," Macey said.

"Do you think they know?" Zach asked me. "Your mom and Joe, do you think they suspect Edwards is dirty?"

"I'm not sure he is," I said with a shrug. "But I don't like him. And I don't like . . . it. In any case, there's no telling who we can trust." I took a deep breath and steadied my nerves as I went on. "And that's why we have to go alone."

"Gallagher Girl, let's think about this."

"I have thought about it. And this is it, Zach. This is what comes next. I'm through waiting and hiding. I'm not running or lying low or going to ground or any of the spy terms that can basically be translated as *wait for someone else to do something*. I am tired of waiting."

I looked around, expecting protests, but none came, so I talked on. "Preston's dad asked for me and he mentioned Liz, so I think she's right, and I think this thing is happening. I think the Circle is trying to start World War Three."

"So that's why we call my parents," Bex countered, and I shook my head.

"They have a job, Bex. They have a mission." I took a deep breath and admitted, "Every last one of them is busy tracking down the leaders of the Circle. Whether they realize it or not, they're trying to stop it from that end. And just hearing our voices might be enough to land them in a prison too. So . . . no. I'm going to try to stop World War Three. And I'm asking you to help me."

"Where do we start?" Bex asked.

I felt them all looking at me—waiting for me to say something, do something. It was the way I always looked at my mom or Aunt Abby or Mr. Solomon. I felt them waiting for orders. And I realized they weren't going with me on this quest—they were *following* me. I felt the weight of the responsibility crushing down on me, and my roommates must have sensed it.

"Cam, you're the one who saw where they're holding Preston." Bex was moving toward me. "You're the one who heard what the ambassador had to say. And, Cam, you're the only one of us who has ever been entirely on your own, going after the Circle."

"I got caught," I reminded everyone. Especially myself.

"You *survived*," Bex told me, emphasis on the final word, on the only thing that really mattered. "So"—she took a slight step back and crossed her arms—"what are we going to do?"

I felt them waiting, watching, and I wondered if Zach was right—if the two of us would be better off on our own. But it was too late. We couldn't lose my roommates if we tried. They were Gallagher Girls. They would find us.

"Lizzie." I turned to her. "What happens next? I mean . . . what's the next domino?"

"It could be any number of things. I built a model, and it's scanning the Internet for anything that fits with the pattern, and then I'll cross-reference that against—"

"Short version, Liz," Bex reminded her.

"I don't know yet," Liz blurted. "But I will soon. Probably soon. Hopefully soon."

"How soon?" I asked.

"A couple days. Maybe sooner."

"Okay, so in the meantime, we get Preston."

I waited for the objections, the questions, the doubts, but no one said a thing until Bex asked, "What do we know about this prison?"

"Before Joe left, he told me it's a maximum-security facility in the Alaskan arctic," Zach said, taking over. "Very remote. Very extreme. *Very* secure. Only the highest-level terror targets are taken there."

"Because it's so remote?" Liz asked.

Zach shook his head. "Because, officially, it doesn't exist. Prisoners only get sent there if they are never supposed to leave."

I didn't want to look at Macey, but I couldn't help myself. I watched her from the corner of my eye, waiting for her to wince or cringe, but she was stoic. Frozen.

"How big is it?" Bex asked.

"Not sure." I shook my head. "The facility was built into the mountain, and I didn't see the whole thing. It was like a maze. I think you're supposed to get lost."

"Do you remember the route you took?" Bex asked, and I smiled.

"Every step."

"Good," Macey said. "There's a gun safe in the basement."

"No." I shook my head.

"But—"

"We can't blast our way in, Macey. No matter how much firepower we bring, they are going to have more. Our only way in is very, very quietly."

"It's not that simple, okay?" Zach shook his head. Frustration poured off him in waves. "You guys don't get it. The temperature and altitude alone make this maybe the hardest target in the country. If you think this is going to be easy, you're crazy."

"Zach's right," Bex said.

"I got out," I said, almost under my breath.

"And you were lucky," he countered.

Until then, I hadn't really considered how miraculous it was. There had been too much adrenaline, too many wild thoughts inside my mind. But that didn't change the fact that I couldn't tell him he was wrong. I could only say, "So I can get in."

"Getting out is different than breaking in," Zach told me.

"It's a prison, Zach. Keeping people in is kind of the idea."

"But—"

"But what?" I asked him.

"But if we get caught, there's no getting out. Maybe ever again."

I thought about what Aunt Abby had told me in Rome, that we couldn't be kids and adults at the same time—that we no longer got to have it both ways. People had already come for Zach. They already wanted me. If we did this it would be official. There'd be no turning back for any of us.

"Okay." Bex rubbed her hands on her thighs, warming them as if in preparation for where we had to go and what we had to do. "We're going." It wasn't an argument. It was an order. And none of us had the strength to defy her. "We're going right now."

Macey walked to a door off the kitchen, threw it open, and switched on the light. Instantly, fluorescents flickered to life, buzzing and glowing and illuminating a massive room filled with rows and rows of shelves covered in skis and down jackets and jumpsuits, cables and tents. Every rich-person toy in the world filled the massive room, and Macey smiled.

"What do we need?"

Chapter twenty-three

Turns out sneaking up on a top secret government prison is far more time-consuming than being invited through the front door.

We left for Alaska the next morning and flew all day. I think the plane belonged to Blackthorne, but Zach didn't explain, and I didn't ask. I just sat in the row behind him while he flew and Bex copiloted. By the time we reached the mountains, she was certain she was certified. I, on the other hand, had had too many bad driver's ed experiences to let her go solo anytime soon. Still, I didn't have the strength to say otherwise.

Step two was a chopper into the forest. I recognized the pilot, a girl named Neha who had been a senior when we were seventh graders. But we didn't exactly catch up. It wasn't exactly the time. Even though it was only seven P.M., we flew under the cover of darkness to the base of a mountain.

And then we were gone, out of the chopper and into the snow. It swirled around us as Neha lifted off, her lights disappearing into a black sky filled with more stars than I had ever seen, leaving us alone in the wilderness with nothing but an uphill climb ahead.

Number of hours we climbed: 6

Number of times Liz fell down: 12

Number of times Liz almost dragged at least three of us down with her: 7

Number of times we said anything about it: 0

Number of moments when I had to wonder if we were making the biggest mistake of our lives: Every single one of them

"We're here."

The way Bex looked around the cave you would have thought it was the Ritz-Carlton. But, in truth, it was a narrow crevice with a dirt floor. Brush covered the entrance. Snow had blown inside, and ice collected in the corners. But it was home, at least for the time being, and I was content to squeeze inside and drop my pack.

"We can light a fire here. They won't see the smoke through the trees, and there's enough ventilation overhead that we don't have to worry about suffocating." Zach pointed up to the ceiling overhead. Cracks ran through the stone, and I could see strips of the starry sky.

"We should get some rest." It was after midnight, and Bex dropped her pack on the ground. "Tomorrow, we have work to do."

Judging from the aches in my back and the sweat in my boots, we'd already done plenty of work today, but I didn't think it was the time to argue. Macey, however, disagreed.

"But—" she started.

Bex cut her off with a look.

"We won't get Preston back by running off half-cocked with no plan, Macey. We get him back by being smart."

"Being smart," Macey repeated.

"Okay." I unfurled my sleeping bag. "Now, get some sleep."

As hard as I tried to sleep, I couldn't. Macey was beside me, too still as she lay on her back, looking up through the cracks in the cave, staring at the stars. They were almost too bright. I wanted to turn them off.

Bex slept, and Liz, worn out as she was, crashed with her boots still on. I wondered where my mom and Mr. Solomon were. I wanted to know if they'd approve of what we were doing.

I saw a shadow move near the doorway, inching down the walls. So I pulled my sleeping bag around my shoulders and, silently as I could, I followed.

"Go to sleep, Gallagher Girl," Zach said. He didn't turn to face me. He just leaned against the cave's entrance, staring at the mountain peak that loomed overhead. He stared so intently at it that I wondered if he had X-ray vision and was trying to see what lay inside. Or maybe he was just trying to see tomorrow.

"I can't sleep," I told him.

"You should try."

"And you're out here not taking your own advice because . . ." I didn't try to finish. I just wrapped the sleeping bag around his shoulders and melted into his arms, rested the back of my head on his chest and leaned against him, staring up at the sky.

"I never knew there were this many stars."

"I can't see them," he told me. His breath was warm on my neck, and he kissed the soft skin at the base of my hair. "I just see you."

"That's one of your cheesier lines," I told him but didn't move to make him stop.

"It's the altitude," he told me. "I don't have enough oxygen in my brain."

"I see." I sighed as his kisses moved higher.

His arms grew tighter around my waist, and for the first time in hours, I wasn't cold. I didn't shiver. I was safe there in that moment and I wanted it to last forever. But it couldn't. From the depths of the cave, I heard Liz coughing in her sleep.

"We shouldn't have let her come," I said.

"If it were up to me none of you would be here." Zach stopped kissing me. He turned me to face him. "You know this is crazy, right?"

"Preston would do it for us," I said.

"Would he?" I couldn't tell if it was a rhetorical question or not until Zach said again, "Would he really?"

I shook my head and looked back at the top of the mountain. It was below zero, and I shivered even in my insulated clothing. I was half a world away from my summer vacation, but the memories I didn't have were always there, coursing under the surface. No matter how many times I tried to claim them, they slipped away. The harder I tried, the faster they shot out of my reach, so I didn't try to grab them then.

"I don't know how to say it, Zach, but . . . last summer. I think he saved my life."

"They may not come for him, Cammie. He's probably safe in there. And . . ." Zach trailed off. Something in his face told me he didn't want to finish. Something in my gut told me he had to.

"And what?"

"What if he's supposed to be in there? What if Preston *is* dangerous?"

I pulled away. Maybe I had to look at him more squarely, or maybe it felt a little like I was temporarily touching a stranger.

"This is Preston we're talking about, Zach. Dangerous isn't the word I'd use to describe him."

"And people are never more than they appear?"

"I can't leave him in there," I said. "Not if we might need him."

"He's Circle, Cammie. He's the next generation."

"He's not."

"He is," Zach said. A cloud passed overhead, and a shadow crossed his face. "I know he is, because I am too."

"No," I said.

"You know what my earliest memory is?" he asked with a sad, quick laugh. "My mom used to sing me this song—about kings and knights and horsemen. All my life, I thought it was just a song—just something mothers sing to little boys. But it wasn't, Cammie. It was about the government. Coups. Power. I wasn't old enough to talk yet, and I was already learning who to hate, and how to burn them to the ground."

"Mothers sing songs, Zach. It doesn't mean—"

"I wonder what kinds of songs Preston's father sang to him." Zach raised his eyebrows. "I wonder if he's lying in a cell humming them to himself right now."

I should have said something—done something. He was in a dark place, there in the moonlight. But before I could say a word, Zach took a deep breath and looked up at the fortress. "I wonder if I should join him."

"No," I snapped and reached for Zach's hand. "You don't get to talk that way."

"But—"

"But your mom and Dr. Steve were in my head ten weeks ago and you're not afraid of me. So you don't get to be afraid of yourself. Not now."

"But—"

"Kiss me, Zach." I pressed up against him, cold and alone. I didn't want to fight. I wanted to be warm and safe again. "Kiss me." I brushed my lips across his mouth, lightly at first, teasing. Tasting. And then his lips parted and the moment was over.

Neither of us was thinking about the past.

Chapter twenty-four

I woke because I was freezing. I might have slept forever, there on that hard ground, had I not sensed that something was missing. Something was wrong.

Someone.

As quickly as I could, I pulled on my boots; but I didn't bother calling out his name. Zach wasn't in the cave, I knew it. He wasn't outside gathering wood or securing our perimeter. I already knew where he was—what he was doing. And so I ran faster, out of the dry cave and into the snow. I pushed against trees and climbed over rocks, following the tracks, cursing that he hadn't even woken me to say good-bye. And when I reached the tree line beneath the icy fortress overhead, I knew exactly what I was going to see:

A lone figure walking through the snow, hands held high above his head in surrender.

I thought about our plan, but also about what he'd said the night before—that maybe he belonged inside that prison too.

"Zach—" I wanted to yell, but in truth the word was nothing but a whisper. We were already out of time.

A door was sliding open on the mountain. Men in white jumpsuits carrying rifles were running down the icy banks, their sights never wavering from the person who was walking toward them, yelling, "I'm Zach Goode. And I'd like to turn myself in."

One could say it was the cold light of morning that made me see things so differently. But at the top of the world in the middle of winter, there wasn't that much light to begin with. An eerie gray filled the sky, and I couldn't help myself; I glanced around, expecting Zach to be there, forgetting he was gone.

Covert Operations Report

Operatives McHenry, Baxter, Sutton, and Morgan joined Zachary Goode for a high-risk, potentially high-reward operation in the Alaskan arctic.

The Operatives also REALLY wished they'd packed extra socks.

By late afternoon, the sunlight was fleeting. Shadows spread across the glistening white plain that stretched between the line of trees where my roommates and I lay on our stomachs, looking up at the fortress above.

"It's kind of beautiful," Liz said, her gaze sweeping over the vista.

"It won't be when that gets here." Bex pointed to the

horizon. Clouds churned, blocking our view of the distant peaks. I could imagine the swirling winds and blowing snow of the coming storm.

A hundred yards of open ground, just snow and ice and some of the most highly calibrated motion sensors and trip wires in the world, stood between us and the compound. Zach's footsteps from that morning were barely visible, filled in by blowing snow.

"What's the time?" Bex asked, even though we all knew the answer.

"Showtime." I looked into the sky. A dark spot was on the horizon just ahead of the ominous clouds. I kept my gaze glued to the helicopter that was no doubt bringing agents to interrogate Zach inside the mountaintop fortress.

"Okay, Lizzie. Are you sure you're okay staying here by yourself? It will be totally dark in an hour. If we're not back by then, I guess . . ."

"Cam," Liz started slowly, "if this takes more than one hour, then my being alone out here is the least of our problems. Now, go," she said, and none of us had to be told twice.

The helicopter grew lower the closer it got to the prison, so we set off running across the open ground beneath the whirl of the spinning blades and the cover of the blowing snow. We'd bleached the gear we'd found in the safe house until everything was white, and we almost blended into the wilderness, bolting over rocks and across ice, up the steep cliffs to the very vent shaft I'd emerged from less than a week before.

On the side of the mountain, a massive door began to rise up out of the ground, opening to allow the helicopter to land inside the fortress.

"Door closing in four-three-two—" I started.

"The charges?" Bex asked Macey, who handed her a tiny pack of explosives that we attached to the grate the prison had secured over the airshaft.

She nodded. "Done."

"Then, fire in the hole," Bex said, and the three of us threw our hands over our heads as a subtle pop filled the air. Plumes of smoke and snow blew into the wind, but it was almost untraceable in the quickly coming darkness.

"Okay, Cam," Bex told me. She shot a cable, sent it spiraling to the top of the shaft. "After you."

I know air ducts and secret passageways. I'm not even a little bit claustrophobic or afraid of spiders. But the darkness that surrounded me then was unlike any that I had ever felt or seen.

I'd been there—in that very shaft—just days before. But then there had been fear and adrenaline. The first time I'd been running away. Now I was climbing *toward*. I don't expect most people to understand the difference, but there is one. I didn't just have to survive—I had to carry. And that made the climbing all the harder. There was time in that quiet place to think, to worry—a nagging, lingering voice that warned that maybe, just maybe we weren't doing the right thing. Maybe we would be too late.

But then the shaft leveled off, and soon I was on my stomach, crawling through the hot air of the prison. Sweat beaded my brow, but I crawled on until I was looking down through a small grate, staring at the same room of monitors I'd seen my last time there.

Then, on one of the screens, I saw him. Preston was lying on the concrete floor of his cell, motionless. And for a second I thought we were too late—that he was injured. Or worse.

But then I realized his feet were tucked beneath his bed. I watched as, slowly, he brought his chest off the floor. His fingers rested lightly behind his ears as he brought his right elbow to his left knee. Down again. Left elbow to right knee. Repeat.

Preston was working out.

Preston wasn't giving up.

Also, Preston kind of looked like a hottie.

But that wasn't the most important thing right then.

I craned my head and looked behind me. Macey couldn't see the screen. She didn't know what I was looking at, and I didn't want to risk her seeing Preston and making a sound, getting careless.

Beneath us, a guard sat watching the monitors, completely ignorant of our presence.

"Guard Station A," a scratchy voice said through a speaker in the room below. The guard reached for a microphone.

"Guard Station A reporting."

"The interrogation team is here," the voice said. "We're ready for the boy."

I watched the guard push a button. I heard a haunting sound, metal on metal as a door opened. And then, through the vent beneath me, I saw Zach walking down the hall.

His lip was swollen and his hands were bound. He wore the same kind of jumpsuit the ambassador had died in, and his feet were bare. The message was clear: *You're free to try to run away, but you'll freeze to death before you make it.*

The guard beneath me stepped into the hall, and that was all the opening I needed. As quickly and quietly as I could, I lowered myself into the office. There were buttons and switches, the same camera feeds that I'd seen my first time there. I walked through the tiny room, not making a noise. Bex and Macey followed.

I heard Zach's voice say, "Well, hello. I remember you from this morning. I was hoping we would meet again."

"Why's that?" a guard said.

"So I could do *this*," Zach told him. I stepped into the hall just in time to see Zach haul back and head-butt the guard, knocking him to the floor.

There was another guard with him, of course. I wondered which of the two men had split Zach's lip, but it wasn't the time to ask.

"Why, you—" guard number two started. He pushed Zach hard against the wall and drew his hand back to punch, but the hand never moved forward. The man whirled as if to question why.

"Hello there," Bex said, and then she slapped him hard across the face. Not a punch. Not a kick. It was an old-fashioned slap, and the man looked almost amused for a moment before the strength slipped out of his limbs and he crumbled to the floor.

The other guard was struggling to his feet, but Macey was already on him, attaching yet another Napotine patch to the back of his neck.

"Is that all?" Bex asked.

"For now," Zach said, then he looked at me. He smirked. "You're late."

I grabbed his hand. "Let's go."

I didn't want to split up. I didn't want to let him go. But being a spy is at least fifty percent doing unpleasant things, and Zach and I were the only ones who had any kind of home-court advantage.

In sixty seconds the people waiting on Zach would wonder why he hadn't reached the interrogation rooms, which, if I remembered correctly, were just fifty yards away.

In a minute and a half they'd try—and fail—to get the guards on the radio. And, of course, at any time a patrol could sweep the corridor, a camera or sensor could tell someone that something wasn't quite right. Time wasn't on our side, in other words, so neither of us wasted a second arguing. We knew Preston was there, and we knew he was alive, and that was the only thing that any of us allowed to matter.

"Did you see him?" Macey asked Zach.

"No," Zach said. "But I heard the guards talking. He's down that way."

"Okay," I said. "Macey, you're with me."

And away we went, carefully moving down the branching corridor while Bex and Zach went the other way.

Most of the cells were empty.

In one I saw a sleeping man who weighed at least three hundred pounds.

In another I saw a woman with red hair. She watched me, silent, as if my presence in her window were completely routine.

"Here!" Macey said. She was reaching for the door, saying, "Preston!" But the door didn't budge.

"Lizzie," I said through the comms unit. "It's cell seventeen."

In a moment, I heard Liz say, "Accessing prison system and . . ."

"Any minute now," Macey prompted.

"Open!" Liz yelled, proud of herself.

The door popped open, and Macey rushed inside.

"Preston, are you okay?" she asked, but Preston just stared at us as if he wasn't quite sure whether or not he was losing his mind.

"Are you here to rescue me, or is this some freaky mind experiment?"

"Rescue," I said with a nod.

Preston smiled. "Then let's go."

Macey took his hand and dragged him out of the cell. As soon as we stepped into the hall, a guard rounded the corner and Macey dropped to the ground, knocking the man's feet out from beneath him. Another guard followed so closely behind that they became tangled together, falling. And I had the Napotine patches out and ready. Neither rose again.

Macey reached for Preston's hand. "This way." She started down the darkened corridor, but Preston held back.

"Is my dad down there?" he asked. Hope shone through his eyes, and I was certain he didn't have a clue about his father's fate. I knew because it was the same look I had been seeing in the mirror for years.

"We've got to go, Preston," I told him and put my hand on his back.

"Is he meeting us outside?"

"Yeah," I said, but Macey just looked at me. Her eyes were wide, and she shook her head, confused. She didn't understand what I knew. That he might not be able to stand—much less run—if we told him the truth. He might lose the ability to think, much less follow orders. There were things we needed out of Preston still, and that meant Preston needed a lie.

"Come on," I told him. "The others are waiting for us." Then I pushed him out the door.

Chapter twenty-five

QUESTIONS I REALLY COULDN'T STOP ASKING MYSELF
(EVEN THOUGH I REALLY, REALLY WANTED TO):
(A list by Cameron Morgan)

- Exactly how many highly trained government operatives were in that building (and about to be chasing us)?

- How were we supposed to tell Preston his father wasn't waiting for us safely outside—that he wasn't going to see his dad in a few minutes? That he was never going to see his dad ever again?

- When had I become someone who could tell a lie like that?

- Did I really want to go back to being someone who couldn't?

We were only inside for fifteen minutes. Not a second more. And yet there, at the top of the world in the middle of winter, that was long enough for the sky to descend into black.

The wind was stronger too, colder. I knew the storm was upon us, because I felt the snow blowing against my face, white streaking through the darkness, and I knew we were almost out of time.

"It's good to see you, Pres," Bex said, taking his hand and pulling him from the entrance of the narrow shaft I'd found just days before. She handed him a pair of extra boots and a coat that matched the one Zach had already put on.

"You too, Bex." Preston put his hands on his hips, out of breath already. It didn't matter how many sit-ups he'd been doing, at that altitude, there was a limit to how far and how fast anyone could run.

"You okay?" Zach asked, and I kissed him—fast and hard, not needing it to linger, just so happy to see him free. Behind us, I could still hear the screaming sirens, the flash of the swirling lights.

"Let's go," I said.

The snow blew harder as we ran down the icy, steep incline.

I saw the main doors to the facility start to open, and I knew it was just a matter of minutes before that mountain would be swarming with guards. Zach and Bex must have known it too, because they sprinted off, not waiting while Macey and I dragged Preston along.

"Now?" Liz's voice rang in my ear, and I looked at Macey, who nodded.

"Now," I said.

"Fire in the hole!" Liz cried, and a split second later a charge ricocheted off the mountain. In the cold, thin air the sound echoed. A puff of smoke and snow blew up from the entrance of the facility, and the doors that had been opening stopped cold. No guards were coming out that way. At least not for a little while.

"Thank you, Dr. Fibs, for your lecture on the strategic placement of explosive charges," Macey said. She looked at Preston, expecting him to appreciate a well-placed explosive charge when he saw one, but he was too cold. Too terrified. Besides, I forced myself to remember, Preston was never trained to be like us.

"Here." I stripped off my hat and put it on his head. We'd come too far to lose Preston to hypothermia now.

"Cammie"—Preston's lips trembled as he spoke—"where's my dad?"

"He'll meet us when we get there," I told him.

"Get where?" Preston asked.

I honestly don't know what I would have told him—what we could have said—but there wasn't any time to say anything, because right then Zach and Bex came bursting around a massive arrangement of boulders, each of them behind the controls of a snowmobile that we'd planned to "borrow" from the facility.

"Come on!" Zach yelled, and neither Macey nor I had to be told twice.

We ran toward them. Macey and Preston hopped on behind Bex, squeezing together.

Liz was screaming in my ear, begging, "Please tell me you guys are clear?"

"Not yet," I said and jumped on Zach's snowmobile just as, overhead, there were cries from more guards, shadows moving in the blowing snow.

Zach turned, and in a flash we were flying down the mountain.

I wasn't sure at first if it was the speed of the snowmobile or if the storm was just picking up, but the snow burned as it blew. My eyes stung, and I struggled to keep them open, so I didn't try. I just buried my face against Zach's shoulder, fighting against the cold.

"You okay?" Zach yelled and, numbly, I nodded, even though he couldn't see me.

"Guys!" Liz's voice was loud and clear in my ear. "You're about to have company. Lots of company!"

I craned my head back and squinted, trying to see through the storm. There were headlights behind us. More snowmobiles. More guards. And guns. They would have lots of guns, and they wouldn't aim to wound.

We weren't in training anymore. The stakes and the bullets were real. It was only February, but I couldn't shake the feeling that we were already on the far side of graduation.

"Guys . . ." Liz yelled again, impatience ringing through her voice, *"are you clear?"*

I glanced behind me one more time. We hadn't gone as far as I'd liked. There was too little space between us and the top of that mountain, but a shot rang out then. Zach swerved. And I knew what the answer had to be.

"Go!" I yelled.

Through the comms unit, I heard Liz say one final time, "Fire in the hole!"

And then the explosion happened. Small at first. It wasn't the size of the charge that mattered, Dr. Fibs had taught us. It was the placement. And Liz had placed that third round perfectly.

Looking back I saw the white plumes of snow fly up on the hillside. The men didn't even really notice until the rumble began, a low moan that came too long after the charge itself to be a part of the initial blast.

No. This was something different. Not man-made. This was Mother Nature's way of keeping people off her mountains.

At first, the snow shifted slowly, settling into place. But then it started to grow faster and faster, stronger and stronger, like a tide that swept between us and the men giving chase. Within moments, the mountain was moving—sliding. The avalanche grew and grew, opening like an abyss, cutting us off from the men who had no choice but to turn back. But the tide kept growing faster, threatening to overtake us too.

"Hold on," Zach yelled. He stood, sending the snowmobile up a narrow, ramp-like rock, shooting us into the blowing snow and raging storm, catapulting us into the dark.

Chapter twenty-six

The jump didn't kill us. At least, my first thought was that we hadn't died. But I didn't let myself get too cocky about the situation. After all, we might have been off the mountain, but we were anything but out of the woods.

Covert Operations Report

The Operatives utilized a highly controversial, yet effective, exit strategy dubbed "the blow stuff up and run approach" by Operative Baxter.

Operative Sutton was quick to point out that blowing stuff up is perhaps her greatest gift.

Once they reached the bottom of the mountain the Operatives were able to make contact with their Emergency Extraction Team.

What the Operatives didn't know was exactly who the Emergency Extraction Team might be.

"Are we sure about this?" I asked Zach, low and under my breath.

"I'm sure," he said.

I'd never seen a night so black (much less at seven o'clock). But so far north in the middle of winter, the clear sky was like a blanket that couldn't keep us warm. A crescent moon hung overhead, and I cursed its light beneath my breath. At that particular moment, darkness was our friend.

Bex leaned against a tree, her head listing to one side. I expected her to be up and pacing, securing our perimeter, cursing the ticking clock. But she sat perfectly still on the cold ground, waiting.

"Bex?" I asked. "You okay?"

"Right as rain, Chameleon." She flashed me her trademark grin. "Just enjoying the scenery."

Macey had her arm around Liz, who was shivering. Preston didn't ask about his father again. Instead, he stared, wide-eyed, across the frozen waters of the lake, almost like we'd pulled him from a dream and he was tempted to go back to sleep. But Zach kept his eyes on the night sky, watching.

"What if we're at the wrong rendezvous point?" I asked.

"We aren't."

"But—"

He pointed into the distance, and then I heard it: a low rumbling hum. It looked almost like a bird was flying low over the tree line, but it was too big for a bird.

The lights were off. The pilot was going on instruments and

moonlight and sheer force of will as the small plane touched down on the snow-covered ice, gliding on skis toward us.

Zach turned to the group. "Let's go."

We hunched low and ran across the ice. Liz slid and fell, and Macey reached for her, half-carried her toward the plane.

"Okay, Zach," I said as we got closer, "are you sure that we can trust this guy?"

"I don't know," a boy said, throwing open the plane's side door and looking down. "Can you?"

"Grant?" I asked. He must have heard the uncertainty in my voice. It had been almost two years since I'd seen him, after all. I thought back to the semester when a small contingency of students from the Blackthorne Institute came to our school. It seemed like another lifetime, and I stood for a moment, paralyzed, wondering exactly how we had gotten so far away from school dances and spying on boys.

Someone opened the copilot's window. "Come on, Cammie."

"Jonas?" Liz cried.

The boy winked. "We're here to rescue you."

The plane was small, but we all fit—even if just barely.

"Hang on," Grant told us as he turned the plane on the ice and started building up steam. We bounced and rocked. The wind shifted, and it felt like we were going to topple over before we even took flight.

"It's going to be close!" Jonas yelled when we finally left the ground and headed for the trees.

I could hear the skis scraping against the icy branches. The engines whined and the plane shook, but we kept climbing, rising steadily into the night.

And then the silence came.

We were officially off the grid and in the middle of nowhere. Avalanche or not, the prison guards were going to have a hard time finding us there, and I finally felt myself exhale.

"It's good to see you, buddy." Grant held out a hand, and Zach took it.

"Thanks for coming," Zach told him. He slapped Jonas on the back. And I felt like I'd fallen into an alternate universe. One where Zach had . . . friends.

Neither Grant nor Jonas asked why we were in the middle of nowhere, desperate for a ride. They didn't inquire as to why we had to fly low across the mountains, out of radar range. This was need-to-know at its finest. We weren't going to lie to Grant and Jonas, and they weren't going to lie to us; and we were all perfectly fine with that arrangement.

"Grant?" Bex asked after the plane leveled off. "Does this thing come with a first aid kit?" Her voice was softer than it should have been. Her eyes were glassy, and her skin was sallow.

"Why?" I looked at Bex just as she unzipped her heavy down jacket. Blood stained her shirt, spreading across her shoulder and dripping down her side.

"Sorry, Cam," my best friend whispered. And then her eyelids fluttered and closed, and I felt my whole world descend into black.

Chapter Twenty-Seven

You never know how you're going to react to something. To anything. Tragedy, joy, heartache. They affect us all in different ways in different times and different places. There, a thousand feet in the air, I squinted against the dark stain that was spreading across my best friend's body. I felt the sticky dampness of the blood and watched the way she crumpled, sliding off the plane's narrow seat and onto the floor.

I think I might have yelled.

I think I might have screamed.

I think I might have cried.

But to tell you the truth, I'm not exactly sure what I did. I remember ripping off her shirt and staring at the blood.

"Light!" someone yelled, and soon there was a flashlight shining down on the small hole in Bex's shoulder.

"Bex!" Zach yelled and dove for her. He held her head. "Wake up, Bex. Wake up. Wake up. Wake—"

Someone was crying. It might have been Liz. Or it might

have been me. All I know is that Macey was beside me, a first aid kit in her hands. And I was reaching around Bex's back, feeling the gooey wetness. A gaping hole.

"Exit wound," I said. Zach pulled Bex into his arms and turned her around and I saw blood. So much blood. "That's good. Isn't that good?" I asked but no one really answered.

"We've got to stop the bleeding," Liz was saying, rattling off facts. "Stop the bleeding. Clean the wound."

I'd heard the words in every lecture on emergency medical procedures that the school doctor and Mr. Solomon had ever given, and yet, I didn't really think about them. My hands were flying, moving, absent from my mind as I took the alcohol from Macey's hand and poured it onto Bex's shoulder. I was glad she was unconscious and didn't have to feel the pain.

The gauze bandages were too small—nothing more than glorified Band-Aids—so I stuck them to the entry and exit wounds and unwound my scarf from around my neck, wrapping her body over and over.

"Don't die, Bex," Liz was chanting. "Don't die. Don't die."

"She's not going to die," I said. "Bex won't die," I snapped, knowing that Bex herself would never allow it.

"Bex, wake up!" Zach yelled one more time.

"We've got to get her on the ground," Liz said.

"We've got to get her to a hospital," Preston countered.

Then Bex's eyes fluttered open. She grabbed my hand, held it tighter than I thought possible.

"No," she gasped. "No hospitals."

"But—"

"They'll find me. Find us," Bex said, and I nodded, knowing she was right. I pressed against Bex's wounds.

"I won't let them find you," I promised, and then my best friend drifted away again, her blood still wet and warm on my hands.

Chapter twenty-eight

Grant and Jonas didn't ask how I knew where the lake was. No one debated how much longer we should fly. We stayed in the air as long as we possibly could, and when the sun began to creep over the horizon I pointed to the waters below and told them, "There."

So we landed. Once we were on the ground, Grant insisted on carrying Bex inside, and my friends and I walked toward the cabin, knee-deep in snow in the predawn light.

"What is this place?" Zach asked.

"It's safe," I told him.

"Cam . . ." Zach said, his voice a warning.

"It's a ranch. Grandpa buys his bulls here. The owners only use this cabin for hunting, though. And nothing is in season now. No one is looking for us here. It's safe," I said again, this time the words only for myself.

Liz and Macey and I stood together in a big crude kitchen with canned goods and a propane-powered cookstove. There was a fireplace, and a small bathroom with a shower but no tub, and two bedrooms. One had a set of bunk beds. The other looked like it belonged in an old motel. In every room there were cheap curtains on the windows and no locks on the doors.

Liz was already unpacking computers and unwinding cords. She looked at me. "Power?"

"There's a generator out back," I said but I didn't move.

"Good," Liz said with a nod. "I still have a backdoor into the NSA satellite system, so I can get that up and running. I need to check on the model, see if there are any headlines. And—"

"Liz." I tried to stop her, but she just turned on me, a raw kind of desperation in her eyes.

It was neither panic nor grief but rather a very grown-up sense of urgency as she told me, "I'm going to find the next domino, Cammie. This thing, I know it's not my fault. Not really. I know I didn't sink that tanker or blow up that bridge, but if someone is doing this based on an idea I had—based on my *ideas*"—she said again, and I knew that that was the hardest part. For someone like Liz, ideas were sacred—"then I've got to stop it." She stood up a little taller. "Then I *will* stop it."

And I knew right then she would.

When Zach emerged from one of the bedrooms, Macey said, "How is she?"

Zach looked down at the ground. "She's still out. I thought she might wake when we moved her, but . . ."

"That's okay," I said. "There's no sign of fever and her pulse is strong. She is strong. She'll be fine."

"She'll be fine," Zach repeated. Then he shook his head and leaned against the cold stove.

Outside, the sun was rising higher, and, gradually, the cabin filled with an almost iridescent glow, like it was coming back to life. But then a voice cut through the haze, asking, "Is he here?"

Preston.

I know it sounds crazy, but I'd almost forgotten about Preston until he looked around the cold cabin, then back at me. "Is my father here, or are we meeting him somewhere else?"

I didn't rush to answer. The truth was just a series of lies I couldn't bring myself to tell: That he shouldn't worry. That things would be okay. That his father didn't suffer. But I didn't want to say any of those things because, for years, I hadn't wanted to hear them.

"He's not coming, is he?" Preston said at last.

"No," Macey admitted.

"Is he . . ." Preston started but trailed off. I couldn't blame him. We were all trained spies, and even we didn't have the strength to finish that particular sentence. "Why isn't he coming? Macey?" He looked at her, but she couldn't face him. "Someone tell me something! Cammie?"

"I'm so sorry, Preston," I said, coming toward him. I took his hands. "I'm so sorry."

I was maybe the only person in the room who knew what he was feeling, but the emotions were too raw for me. When he pushed away, I didn't protest—didn't follow. My own wounds were too sore. But I also knew that I was the only one who'd been there. I was the only one who had found my way out.

"My father is dead," Preston said slowly, almost like he was admitting something he was ashamed of. "Of course he's dead. Wasn't that what you were trying to tell me in Rome—that people like my dad were dying?"

"Preston," Macey started, but he was only looking at me.

"How did he die?" Preston struggled to keep his voice from cracking. He was still slightly frozen and totally numb, and he was trying to hold it all together, trying not to break down and be the weak link as he looked at me. "Do you know how he died?"

I wasn't aware I was biting my lip until I tasted the blood. I nodded slowly. "He was shot. In custody. A few days ago."

"In custody?" Preston asked like he was trying to wrap his mind around the facts, put them all in perspective. "In that place?"

He pointed at the mountain that was, by then, a thousand miles away.

"Yes," I said. "He was there."

"So he died," Preston said again, like he was still trying the words on for size, trying to make them fit. "Was it your mom?" he asked Zach.

"We don't know," Zach admitted as if the question wasn't offensive at all. And I guess when your mom is a psychotic terrorist it isn't. "Cammie was there but she didn't get a good look at the gunman. He could have been acting on Catherine's orders. Or maybe the other members of the Inner Circle wanted to eliminate him before he could talk. We aren't sure which."

Preston whirled on me. "You saw it happen? You were there?"

"It was dark. I was in the other room, but . . . yes. I was there."

"What were you doing there?" Preston asked.

"He asked to see me. I thought I was going to see you, but it was him instead. He told them I was the only person he would talk to."

"Why?" Preston asked.

I shook my head. "He said he wanted to talk to me . . . about the Circle. And he asked me to keep you safe. But when I saw what happened to him, I knew you were never going to be safe in there."

"And I'm supposed to be safe out here?" Preston yelled. The shock was wearing off, taking its toll. All that was left was fear and grief and terror. "Why did they arrest me?"

"The Circle," Macey said. "It's kind of a family business. It's *your* family business."

But Preston didn't take the time to process this. He fired back, "Do you think I'm one of the bad guys?"

"No!" Macey reached for him, but Preston pulled away.

"Maybe I am." A darkness filled his face. The truth about his father was seeping in, bleeding through his outer layers. "I could kill someone."

"No," Macey said. "You couldn't."

Preston pulled a chair out from the table and sank into it. It was like he no longer had the strength to stand.

"Where is my mother?"

"We don't know exactly," I told him. I wanted to keep the

facts plain and straight and simple. He'd already heard too much to process any more. "We think she's safe."

"Are you sure?" Preston asked.

"The Circle is kind of a 'by blood' situation," Zach explained. "It's not the kind of thing you marry into."

The wind blew and the cabin moaned, and the look in Preston's eyes made my stomach churn. I thought I might throw up.

"I'm not surprised about my father." Preston was tracing circles on the table. I doubt he even realized he was doing it, but he kept doing it again and again. "He was a member of the Circle," he said as if trying the words on for size. "Should I be surprised?"

He looked at Macey, who shrugged. "Our dads are politicians, Preston. Of course we grew up thinking they might be evil."

"Preston." I risked moving a little closer, sat down at the table and reached for his hand. "When I saw your dad, he told me the Circle leaders are planning something. We think . . . we think they are trying to start World War Three. And he told me *you* can help stop it."

"How?" Preston sounded genuinely confused. "How am I supposed to know how to stop World War Three? That's ridiculous."

"I know how it sounds. It's just . . . have you heard anything? Seen anything? Did your dad give you something for safekeeping or—"

"I don't know anything, Cammie."

"You have to. He told me you did. He—it was his dying breath, Preston. Now, think!"

"Cam." Zach's hand was on my shoulder, but I pushed on. "You know something!"

"No." Preston was rising, shaking his head. "No. No. Just . . . no."

Even though the sun was growing higher, none of us had slept the night before. Stress and fear mixed with exhaustion, and I could sense Preston starting to crack.

Zach must have seen it too, because before I could press again, Zach took his arm. "Come on, Preston. Let's get you some sleep."

I thought I was alone on the porch. Right up until the moment when I felt Zach's arms go around me. There are many advantages to being romantically involved with a spy, and totally spontaneous and unexpected hugging has to be one of them. I leaned against him, felt the warmth of his body against mine.

"You're shaking," he told me. He turned me to face him, ran his hands quickly up and down my arms. "You shouldn't be out here like this."

But it wasn't the cold that shook me. It was shock or fear or maybe just the sensation of adrenaline draining from my body, so I shook harder.

Through the window I saw Preston sitting at the rickety little table, rocking slightly.

"How many will they send?" I asked. "For him." I nodded in Preston's direction.

"You mean the good guys or the bad guys?" he asked.

"Either," I said with a shrug. "Both." Then I had to laugh. "It's getting harder to tell the difference."

Zach shook his head. "I know the feeling." Then he turned, and the sunlight sliced across his face.

"You're bleeding," I said.

I brought my sleeve up to touch the scrape near his hairline, but Zach moved away.

"It's nothing. I'm fine. It's not mine."

"Bex." I exhaled the word.

"She'll be fine," he told me. "I'm fine."

"I don't think I'll ever be fine again."

"Hey." Zach reached for me.

"What are we doing, Zach?" I asked, pulling away before he could surround me in his arms. "What is it all for? Are we really going to stop the Circle? Is that even possible?"

"Yes." I'd never heard Zach's voice so confident and full of strength. But I didn't let myself believe it. I was too busy rambling on.

"What good will it do? What are we supposed to do if we stop them? We can't trust the CIA. The FBI. Where are we supposed to go, Zach? Are there any good guys?"

"Yes." He grabbed me, pulled me close. "You're looking at one."

And then he kissed me, hard and fast. He pulled back. "And when it's over—"

"No." I stopped him. "Let's not think about the future." I kissed him again. "Let's just not think."

Chapter twenty-nine

Light and dark blurred together. Eventually, the sun set and rose again, but I was like a newborn with my days and nights mixed up, and I almost never slept in coordination with the sun. I almost never slept at all. I just stayed by Bex's bedside, listening as she said, "Cammie." Her lips were dry and cracking, and I dabbed at them with a damp cloth.

"I'm here, Bex," I told her. I felt her forehead, but it was cool. No fever, no infection, just a deep and fitful sleep; and I had to hold her down to keep her from tossing too badly and opening up her brand-new stitches, courtesy of Macey—and the Gallagher Academy's intensive emergency medical procedures training.

"We have to find Cammie," she mumbled.

"I'm here, Bex. I'm back," I said, and only then did I realize that a part of her was still looking for me. Part of her might never stop.

"How is she?"

I turned at the sound of the voice.

"The antibiotics in the med kit that Liz brought with us from school were really strong. They've knocked her out. But she's fine," I told Preston. "It's just her shoulder." I said again, "She's fine."

"Do you think I could sit with her?" Preston asked from the doorway. He took a step forward, his hands shoved into his back pockets. "Let me rephrase. I'm going to sit with her. You're going to take a break."

When I stood and walked into the main room, my legs didn't want to work. My head swirled a little, too light on my shoulders. I hadn't eaten. I hadn't slept. I'd done nothing for days but worry and doubt and pray.

A light was flickering in the kitchen. An eerie fluorescent glare filled the room, the bulbs humming and buzzing and clinging to life. Liz lay with her head on the table, laptops sprawled around her, running through lines and lines of code, analyzing news stories and weather patterns—searching for the proverbial needle in the haystack.

I wanted to wake her up and tell her to go get some sleep in a real bed, but I knew there was no use, so I just took a seat beside her and turned one of the laptops to face me, holding my breath as I called up the website I'd been quietly checking for days. There wouldn't be anything, I was certain.

I was wrong.

I couldn't breathe as the website came to life. It was supposed to advertise farm and ranch land for sale in the Sandhills. I still remember my father looking at the site when I was a little girl. He would talk about a future when we would return to Grandma and Grandpa's and never leave. When we would be safe and sound in Nebraska. All spies have an exit plan, an anonymous city or stretch of abandoned beach. My father was going to have a rock house and a natural spring, good fences and enough horizon so that the spy in him would always be able to see what was coming.

I blinked twice and read the ad again.

M&M properties offering twenty acres for sale. Excellent condition. And a phone number I'd never seen before.

It had been years since my mom had told me about it, put the plan into place. It was just for emergencies, she had said, just in case we ever got separated. Because, deep down, I think we'd both always known something like that was coming.

I read the lines again.

M&M properties: Matthew Morgan.

Twenty acres: Two agents.

Excellent condition: They were fine.

And a phone number that—to anyone else—wouldn't work. But if I added one to every digit, I could finally hear my mother's voice.

I ran to our stash of burner phones and dialed without thinking. I couldn't breathe as the phone rang and rang, and then finally: "Hey, kiddo."

"Mom!" I practically shouted. I was on the verge of crying. "I'm so glad to hear from you. We're—"

"Wise Guy and I are fine," she talked on, not stopping, not caring what I said or how many tears broke through my throat—and I knew she wasn't listening. She probably didn't even have that phone anymore. It was just a recording.

"We're safe. We're closing in on the Delauhunt heir, we think." I heard her take a deep breath, static temporarily filling the line. "I heard what happened at school, sweetheart. And I'm glad you left. You're doing the right thing. I'm so proud of you. But you have to promise me you won't worry about us. Wise Guy and I . . . we'll keep each other safe. You girls . . . you do the same, okay? Keep each other safe."

I thought about Bex's blood, her fitful dreams. And, finally, I thought about how easily we all could have died on that mountain.

"I won't use this number again, and you should destroy your phone too. We have the dead drop. Use it if you need it. But, sweetheart, just promise you'll be careful. You're doing the right thing," Mom said again.

"And, kiddo. Happy birthday."

Birthday. I had forgotten my own birthday. Sometime in the past week I'd turned eighteen, and I hadn't even realized it. I looked down at the phone in my hand. I knew I was supposed to destroy it immediately, but I couldn't. Instead, I listened to the message again and again and again.

"You're doing the right thing."

I listened until the words lost all meaning, until I became numb to even my mother's voice. I listened until I didn't even hear the words anymore.

You're doing the right thing.

* * *

Zach was in the kitchen. He wore old jeans and had bare feet, and I thought that maybe bacon-frying was a pretty dangerous thing to do without a shirt on, but I didn't say so.

"Gallagher Girl?" He looked at the burner phone I carried in one hand, the SIM card I held in the other.

"It was my mom," I told him.

"What did she say?"

"She's fine," I said, then hurried to add, "*They're* fine. They're closing in on Delauhunt and . . . It was just a message, Zach. She didn't tell me what to do. She just said that I was doing the right thing."

"You are."

"I couldn't tell her about Bex or Preston. I couldn't tell her—"

"Hey." He reached me in one long stride, arms going around me, so strong and sure, and I pressed my cheek against his chest. He smelled like soap and bacon. "Tell me what she said."

So I did. I told him every word, not that any of them mattered. Even Rachel Morgan didn't know what we were supposed to do next.

"I forgot my own birthday, Zach. I'm eighteen now," I said, but I didn't feel like an adult. I felt like a little girl, alone and afraid and desperate for my mother.

"It's going to be okay. Hey." He wiped my tears away. "We're going to be okay."

Here's the thing about being a spy: sometimes all you have are your lies. They protect your cover and keep your secrets, and right then I needed to believe that it was true even when all the facts said otherwise.

"What's going on?" Macey said from the bedroom door. At the sound, Liz stirred and bolted upright.

"Why didn't you wake me up?" Liz asked. She yawned and looked down at the laptop in front of her. Two seconds later, her face went whiter than I'd ever seen it. Her lips trembled, and her fingers froze on the laptop's keys. She looked away, but it was too late. Even without her photographic memory, Liz could never un-see what the computer said.

"This is it." Liz pushed her favorite laptop away with so much strength it would have fallen off the table if Zach hadn't been there to stop it. "It's happening now."

I looked at the screen and read the words aloud for no one's benefit but my own. "'Exiled King Najeeb of Caspia to address protesters outside the United Nations.'"

As much as I wanted to deny what was happening in the world outside our little cabin, I knew there was no use trying to hide. The facts will always find you. And the scarier they are, the faster they travel.

Liz was up and moving across the room. She's always had this habit of bringing her right hand to her mouth, resting her fingertips against her lips while she talks to herself, almost as if learning to read her lips by touch. She was doing it then. She spoke so quickly and so softly that I could barely make out the words.

"This is it. This is happening." Then she seemed to doubt herself. "*Is* this it?"

Liz was walking, but it wasn't with the panic-ridden steps of a caged animal. It was the careful, cautious pacing of a genius who needed time and space to think.

I risked a glance at Zach, but he was quiet, like he didn't want to break whatever trance Liz was in, like he too knew she was our single best chance at stopping the Circle.

Liz paced and talked like it was just another test. Another challenge. She was looking at it like an exercise in probability—cause and effect. It's the physics of human nature, and to truly understand it, one has to be objective and cool. Two things every operative is supposed to be. Two things I was becoming less and less acquainted with all the time.

"Tension," Liz said at last. She was still pacing, though, and I knew the word was meant only for her. "That region is filled with conflict, but the Circle will need to ratchet up the tension. It will have to be something big. And public. Something that is symbolic and practical at the same time."

Some people always want to fight. Some are always looking for a reason not to. And Liz was right: For the Circle to cause World War III, they had to take away any cause for diplomacy and caution.

"It has to be personal," Liz said, finally looking at all of us. It was almost like she'd forgotten we were even there. "Someone has to strike first."

"And by strike you mean . . ." Zach prompted.

"An assassination. The Circle is going to assassinate the king of Caspia."

"Caspia doesn't have a king anymore," Macey reminded her, but Liz just shook her head.

"King Najeeb may be living in exile, but he's still incredibly popular in his home country. If he were to die, then the Caspian government would have a full-fledged revolt on their hands. And the Iranians are banking on a very stable Caspia. That is their largest remaining trade route. If Najeeb dies, then the Iranians will have to move in to stabilize the region."

"And break the Treaty of Caspia . . ." I filled in.

"Exactly," Liz said with a nod.

World War I ignited after the killing of an Austrian duke. World War II began with German troops crossing a border. Sometimes big things start in small ways. And it was easy to imagine what the assassination of a king might lead to.

"We have to stop them."

"We can't move Bex."

"We should move Bex to a hospital."

I wasn't sure who said what, to tell you the truth. The words were a blur. Were they coming from outside or inside my mind? I could no longer tell. The only things I heard for sure were my mother's words coming to me over and over again.

You're doing the right thing.

"Cammie." Liz's voice broke through the fog. "Cammie, what are we going to do? They're going to assassinate the king!"

"No they aren't." I turned to see Bex leaning against the door frame, weak as a kitten. But there was a spark in her eyes again. She was utterly and completely *Bexish* as she said, "They aren't, because we're going to stop them."

Chapter thirty

PROS AND CONS OF DRIVING
CROSS-COUNTRY TO STOP A POSSIBLE
ASSASSINATION ATTEMPT:

PRO: Big elaborate road trips are supposed to be a teenage rite of passage.

CON: Somehow I don't think normal teenage road trips involve buying a van from a dealership called Toothless Joe's Quality Used Vehicles (even though everyone we saw did, in fact, have teeth).

PRO: It is a whole lot easier to continually bounce your Internet access off of various satellites if you are constantly moving into the range of different satellites.

CON: It's pretty hard to remain alluring and attractive to your boyfriend if you spend all your time sleeping and eating and working at sixty miles an hour.

PRO: Knowing you're doing the thing you've been training to do since you were twelve years old.

CON: Knowing in your gut that you might not be ready to actually do it.

———————

I'm not going to say it was the strangest covert task force ever assembled, but it wasn't exactly ordinary either.

"We should go in from the north," Zach said, leaning forward and addressing Macey, who drove.

I looked through the windows at the towering buildings of the Manhattan skyline. The streets were already packed with people carrying picket signs and Caspian flags.

"What do we know, Lizzie?" Bex asked. She held on to the back of the front seat, supporting herself more than she usually would, but she didn't wince or show any kind of pain or fear. She was being brave. I would have settled for her being careful.

"His Royal Highness will be addressing the rally at noon exactly. He will make brief remarks from a stage on the street in front of the UN. There's a little square there for protests and rallies. The NYPD should have the whole area blocked off."

"Is he going inside?" Zach asked.

Liz shook her head. "According to what I've gotten off of the UN servers, he can't. Not really. I mean, technically, the king is a deposed monarch, which means he has no official authority to speak on behalf of Caspia."

I couldn't help myself. I looked at the people who filled the streets, many of them carrying signs with a royal crown on them, pictures of the king. "Yeah. But you'd have a hard time convincing them of that."

We drove as far as we could, then Macey parked the van. We left Liz there to run our comms and do her magic with the computer. As we walked toward the East River, the wind blew harder, and the crowds grew heavier with each passing step.

"Cam," Macey said, "have you heard anything else from your mom?"

I shook my head, but it took me a second to speak. "I put a post on the message board that we know what the Inner Circle is planning. But she may not get it in time. Or she may be too far away or already engaged in another op or . . ."

Hurt.

Dead.

Imprisoned.

I didn't like any of the other possible ends of that sentence, so I didn't say them. No one blamed me. No good would come from saying them aloud.

"I think about the Caspia I knew as a child." A voice came booming through the streets, and my friends and I all stopped to listen. The man's English bore the accent of someone who was raised in the Middle East but educated in the West—America, or England, maybe. And when he spoke, it was like all of New York fell under his trance.

There was no denying it: that was the voice of a king.

"He's here." Until I said the words, I hadn't realized how much I'd been hoping that it all might have been just a false alarm, an easy fix. "Liz, I thought you hacked into Homeland

Security and told them there was a potential terror threat at the UN this afternoon?"

"I did!" she countered. "I gave them enough to shut down half the city. I don't know what's happening."

"I do."

Until then, Preston had been quiet. An observer. A guest. He seemed almost surprised when we all turned to him. "I mean, have you ever seen a politician give up a microphone?" Preston quipped, then shrugged. "I haven't."

And I knew he had a point.

"We're too late," Macey said.

The United Nations was right ahead of us, on the other side of a wide avenue that had been blocked off. Crowds stood between us and the long row of flags from all the participating countries. The flags blew in the wind, the flagpoles standing like a hundred sentries guarding the entrance to the building.

But the people on the street didn't care about the towering glass-and-steel structure. Their eyes were trained upon the small grassy area that had been cordoned off, a man and a microphone centered on the small stage.

"There were hard times," the man said, "but there was hope. There was fear, but there was also courage. I think of the Caspia that I wanted for *my* child, and my heart breaks that Amirah will never know the sunrises over our sea. My soul bleeds to think that all of our children will never know a Caspia without tyranny and fear!"

The crowds erupted in thunderous applause.

"What do we know?" I asked.

"Amirah, crown princess of Caspia," Liz said through our comms units, rattling off enough facts to make Mr. Smith proud; but the time for tests was over. We were never going to be graded again. "She's second in line to the throne."

"No, Liz," Bex countered. "She doesn't have a throne anymore."

"What do we know about the *security situation?*" I asked, this time being more specific.

"We've got to get him out of here," Macey said.

"Zach, talk to me." I turned to the boy who had spent more time with Joe Solomon than any of us, and Zach didn't wait for instructions.

"Since he's not an official visiting dignitary, the Secret Service won't be here. He will have private security and the NYPD."

"Good. Macey, you and Preston go find the cops and his private security detail. Beg, plead—lie if you have to—but get someone to get him off that stage."

"Got it," Macey said. She grabbed Preston's hand, and together they took off, pushing through the crowds.

"Liz, get back into the NYPD database and alert all units in the area that we have possible terror activity. If Homeland Security isn't going to take this seriously, maybe the NYPD will. Let's see if we can't get them to shut this thing down."

"I'm on it," Liz told me.

In my mind, I flashed back to another clear day, another charismatic man behind a microphone while crowds cheered. At the time, Macey's father had been running for vice president, and we'd thought that she was the one the Circle of Cavan was chasing. At the time, Mr. Solomon had spoken about security perimeters—long-range, mid-range, short-range. Zones A, B, and C. And I looked to the horizon.

"What can we do about snipers?" I asked, and Zach scanned the skyline. Clear views and light wind. And even without saying a word, I could see it in Zach's eyes. He didn't like the situation.

He looked at Bex, who shook her head.

"That building puts you on top of three different bus routes. It's a clear shot with great exits. So . . . nothing," she said. "There is nothing we can do about snipers except . . ."

"We've got to get him out of here," I filled in the rest.

On the stage, King Najeeb spoke on, a somber silence sweeping farther through the crowd with every word. "I do not hate the men who burned my father's statues. I have forgiven the mob who dragged my mother from her bed."

I thought of my own mother. Where was she sleeping? And would she wake one night to the feeling of a cold barrel of a gun against her temple?

A limousine and two NYPD police cruisers were pulling around the back of the crowd to a small area behind the stage. I felt a tiny bit of hope that maybe it was working—that he was leaving.

Together, we started pushing through the crowd, trying to make our way to the stage and the man upon it, who kept speaking. If King Najeeb knew the danger he was in, he didn't show it.

"The home I love is gone now, but I do not mourn for it. I pray instead for the promise of a new day, a new era, a new beginning, when peace and love can shine upon all the children of Caspia. A new reign of hope and not of fear, of promise and not of terror. I pray for home. I pray for Caspia. I pray for the future."

Applause filled the streets, followed by chants and cries. King Najeeb stepped away from the microphone and waved triumphantly at the crowd. I felt my heart start to beat again, knowing he was finished. He was okay. But he wasn't safe, and we all knew it. I waited for him to leave the stage, for his guards to hurry him into the waiting car; but the king pushed his guards aside.

"He's a man of the people," I said, citing some article that Mr. Smith had made us read once about all the royals in the world who were living in exile. The former king chose an apartment over a palace, a subway pass over a limousine. And, whenever possible, he liked to walk wherever he went.

The peaceful, easy chanting of the crowd was changing, morphing from song to roar, as the people parted and the king climbed down from the stage, easing out into the crowd as if intending to shake the hand of every person who had gathered there.

"No!" I yelled. "He's got to go! Make him go!" I yelled to no one in particular. My cries were lost in the crowd.

There were guards in dark suits speaking into his ear, but King Najeeb didn't seem to notice them or care. He was shaking the hands of his people. Blessing babies and waving at the masses like a returning, conquering hero.

He walked without a worry or a fear in the world right through the heart of Security Perimeter B—the area that was most dangerous for short-range arms and high-powered explosives.

Was it that thought that made me stop? I don't know. Maybe my subconscious saw the small, abandoned package before the rest of me could process what it meant. Maybe it was Joe Solomon's voice in the back of my head or my father's angel on my shoulder, but in any case I *did* stop.

And I looked at the package on the ground, directly in the king's path.

And I heard my own voice scream, "Bomb!"

Looking back, it was like it happened in slow motion—like running through sand. One moment, I was watching the king stroll through his people, shaking hands. The next there was nothing but a cloud of smoke and terror. People screamed. Children cried. But it all sounded so far away, like a TV blaring in a distant room.

I coughed and squinted. The force of the blow had knocked me to the ground, and my side ached. My hands hurt. It took everything I had to force myself upright.

"Cam!" Zach was yelling. I realized there was static in my ear. The blast must have knocked out our comms units. In the smoke, we were practically deaf and blind.

"Cam!" Bex yelled.

"I'm here!" I said. There was a bleeding woman carrying a child.

A man stumbled through the crowd, his face so covered in blood that I couldn't even tell what damage had been done.

"I'm here," I said, softer, as I pushed against the current of people trying to flee the blast site. I had to see it. The crater where the bomb had begun. The mangled bodies of the guards and the man who was Caspia's only hope for peace.

"And I'm too late."

Chapter thirty-one

Surely that wasn't the longest night of my life, but it felt like it.

Not one of us protested when Liz insisted we stop and clean our wounds in the bathroom of a gas station outside the city. They were inconsequential, really. Scrapes and bruises. I had a pretty nasty cut on my shoulder, but nothing any worse than any of us had had before. We'd been on the perimeter of the blast radius. Ten feet closer to the king, and we wouldn't have been so lucky.

Once we were back in the van, I risked a glance at Zach. No one had tended to his scrapes and burns. No one had tried to. He just kept staring out the window, looking for what, exactly, I didn't really know.

Maybe a way out.

Maybe a chance to turn back time.

We kept the radio of the van turned low. News of the king's assassination swept across the globe. Riots were spreading throughout Caspia and beyond, crossing borders, a whole region on fire. Chaos was the new norm. The world was a powder keg, and I rubbed my sore body, afraid I'd just felt the spark.

We drove all night, heading south along the coastline until I was almost convinced Zach was going to drive us out to sea.

Finally there was a dock with a small ferry that you had to push with a long pole, like it was still 1850. At last there was an island and an overgrown pathway and a house surrounded by tall trees filled with Spanish moss, a massive wraparound porch and a scene befitting Scarlett O'Hara.

"What is this place, Zach?" I asked, but he didn't answer. He just kicked the front door; but it didn't put up a fight, splintering easily, swinging open. Liz carried her computers protectively like there might be an alligator or a monster after her hard drive. But Zach said nothing. He just kept looking at the staircase as if waiting for a ghost to descend from the second floor.

It had been a grand old house once, a mansion. But everything about it had fallen into rubble from decades of disuse and neglect.

"Is this one of Joe's houses?" I waited, but Zach was speechless. "If it's Joe's house, Zach, we probably shouldn't stay. Someone may track us here."

"Not Joe." Zach shook his head.

"But you know it." It wasn't really a question, not a guess. I inched slowly closer. "Whose house is it, Zach?"

"It's safe." He turned. "We'll be safe."

"Zach . . ." I reached for him, but he pulled away and

walked to the corner of the room, measuring his footsteps carefully, listening until one step sounded slightly different from the others. Then he knelt to the floor and removed one of the boards and reached inside to pull out six birthday candles and a G.I. Joe, a rumpled five-dollar bill and an assortment of broken crayons—and only then did I know where Zach had brought us. After all, that wasn't the covert stash of an operative; it was the hiding place of a child.

"This was your mother's safe house," I whispered.

But Zach just looked around the big, dusty rooms that must have been so grand, once upon a time. "No. It was her *house*," he said.

Spies aren't like normal people. No one expects us to have houses and mortgages, tire swings and barbecues on the Fourth of July. But every spy is somebody's child, and I stepped across those dusty floorboards, wondering what kind of place had given birth to the woman we called Catherine.

"This was my room." He looked into the small space. "There were bedrooms upstairs, of course, but I didn't like being alone. I was scared of the dark and the wind and the storms. . . . There were such bad storms."

"Can it be traced to you, Zach? To her?"

"There's natural gas on the property, and the rooms are still lit with gaslight. I think there might be a generator. A water well, but no phone. The whole house is off the grid." Zach gave a gruff laugh. "It doesn't even know there is a grid."

"When was the last time you were here?"

"I don't know. Ten years ago? Maybe longer. She used to talk about fixing it up—making it like it was in its prime. But I don't know how it was. I just know this."

He motioned around the derelict rooms, and I don't know if he meant it or not, but it sounded like he was saying he didn't know anything other than a vagabond way of life. "This is all I know."

"Maybe we shouldn't stay here, Zach," I tried. "We could keep driving."

"You don't get it, Gallagher Girl." He shook his head slowly. "The king is dead. There's nowhere else to go."

I grew up in an old mansion. I know the chill that creeps through stone walls, the sounds a roof can make in a hard wind. But that night was different. Everything creaked and moaned. When the rain started, it fell in heavy waves, beating against the house and dripping through the ceiling. There was a steady, even ping as fat drops fell on the keys of the old piano. And the longer the storm pounded outside, the more I expected the house might blow right off its foundation and out into the waves.

There must have been debris in the chimney, because when we built a fire, smoke backed into the house, filling it with an eerie haze. We propped open the front door, and for a while the smoke mixed with the wet wind while Preston and Macey surveyed the contents of the kitchen. Liz was unpacking equipment, and Zach stoked the fire.

But I just sat at the bottom of the stairs, rubbing my palms against my jeans, dried blood smearing onto dark denim, wondering, *Is that it? Is it really over?*

"What happens now?" I looked up to find Bex leaning against the banister, looming over me. It was like she'd read my mind.

"You should get some sleep, Bex. We'll probably need to change your bandages and—"

"I'm not talking about my bloody bandages," she said, then grinned. "No pun intended."

"Look, Bex . . ." I started. Suddenly, I felt so tired, so worn.

"No, *you* look. This isn't the end," she told me. "You think I got shot . . . for *this?*" Bex snapped. "I'm a spy, Cam. I was born to do this—to be this. It's in my blood. And I will do it until the day I die. It's who I am," my best friend said, then leveled a glare at me. "The thing I don't think you realize is . . . it's who you are too."

"I know."

"No." Bex shook her head. "You don't. If you did, you never would have spent half of our sophomore year dating Josh. You wouldn't be freaked out at the thought of graduation. You would know what life after spy school means. It means this, Cam. *This.* And you are better at it than anyone that I have ever known. Now, get up. And tell us what comes next."

But I didn't move.

"Okay. Let's have it." She held out her hand, waggled her fingers.

"What?"

"You know what," my best friend told me. "Hand it over."

I didn't ask again. I just reached into my pocket and pulled out the list I'd been carrying around for weeks.

"There." Bex pointed at the paper. "William Smith. Gideon Maxwell. Two names, Cam. There are only two names left!"

"I know, but . . ."

"But what?" Bex demanded.

"But the king is dead, Bex." I felt silly pointing it out, almost disrespectful saying the words aloud. "We didn't stop the assassination. We couldn't—"

But Bex didn't wait for me to finish. She spun and yelled across the room.

"Liz, has it started yet?" Bex asked. "Have the Iranians invaded Caspia?"

Liz sat at her computers. She didn't say a word; she just shook her head. No.

"Then there's time to bloody well stop it!"

I knew she was right. Of course she was. Bex was always right. She knew me better than I knew myself. But then again, isn't that a best friend's job?

"So tell me what comes next," Bex demanded.

I looked up at her for a long time, thinking, praying. My voice was scratchy and distant. It wasn't like my own when I stood and started to speak.

"Liz, when we get a secure line let me know. I've got to try to contact Mom and Abby." Macey and Preston came in from the kitchen, and I looked around the group. "As for the rest of us, we're going to try to get some sleep. Regroup. And first thing tomorrow morning, we're going to figure out what happens next."

I meant it in that moment. I really did. I thought we would sleep for a few hours and wake up to a new day filled with new possibilities. I thought the morning would bring change. But I should have known that it doesn't take that long for change to happen—it takes a second. A moment. In a single breath, reality as you know it can simply fall away.

When I heard a sound on the porch I thought it was the wind rattling the shutters. It felt like the world and its troubles were blowing straight to our door, so I looked at my friends in turn and said, "Okay, everybody, get some sleep, and tomorrow we'll figure out how to stop the Circle."

"Oh." A laugh filled the room. "Maybe I can help with that."

I spun to look at the woman who stood silhouetted in the door. Wind gusted around her, and bits of hair blew across her face, framing her dark eyes as she looked at Zach and said, "Hello, sweetheart. Sorry to disturb you, but I believe you have a walk-in."

Chapter Thirty-two

Maybe you've never heard the term "walk-in." If you're reading this, though, you probably have. You probably know that it's the term spy agencies use for when rival operatives come in out of the cold. It's a phrase that brings to mind hope and fear in equal measures. *This could be big,* you think. *This could be nothing,* you know. But whatever the case, it is never, ever something that you ignore or disregard.

And that's why we all sat staring at the door, every one of us gaping at the woman who stood there.

In a flash, Zach was moving toward her, but Catherine held her hands up in surrender.

"I come in peace," Catherine said.

None of us believed her.

Zach was almost to his mother, who reached out as if to hug him or touch his face.

"I missed you, darling," Catherine told him. "You've grown into such a handsome young—"

But his mother didn't finish because, just then, I rushed past Zach, toward the woman who had captured me—kidnapped me. I didn't think as I pulled back my fist and punched with all my might. I felt pain and satisfaction in equal measure as I watched Catherine crumble, unconscious, to the ground.

REASONS I TOTALLY, COMPLETELY, ABSOLUTELY WAS NOT GOING TO SLEEP THAT NIGHT (NO MATTER HOW MUCH EVERYBODY TOLD ME I HAD TO):
(A list by Cameron Morgan)

- Despite popular belief, hitting someone with a closed fist actually hurts the hitter almost as much as the hittee.

- One of the little bones in my hand was technically broken.

- It's really hard to sleep when your ice pack keeps leaking all over your pillow.

- The only thing worse than getting injured is Liz's becoming your self-appointed nurse and, consequently, hurting you many, many more times while changing your bandages.

- The look in Zach's eyes when he saw his mother.

- The look in Zach's mother's eyes when she saw me.

- Knowing that an assault on a walk-in was in violation of at least three rules of the Geneva convention.

- Remembering that I totally and completely didn't care.

———————

"What is she doing here?" I heard Liz's voice as soon as the sun came up. Creeping toward the stairs, I saw her below, pacing like a tiny blond blur. The rain must have stopped and the chimney must have cleared, because the air was warm and dry—almost cozy—as I walked down the stairs.

"What does she want? Presumably not to kill us . . . because we're not dead." Liz was rattling off the facts at ninety miles per hour. "Let's say we're looking at a double-agent situation. She's come to infiltrate us and send our plans back to her bosses."

"She doesn't have bosses," Bex said, but Liz rattled on.

"Maybe she really is a walk-in. Maybe she has information for us and we can—"

"We can't listen to her, Liz," Bex said.

"But—" Liz started, until Zach cut her off.

"She's just as dangerous in here as she is out there. You got that?" he asked. He looked at Bex and Liz in turn. "Do you understand?"

Macey took a deep breath and crossed her arms. "Well, I vote we bind her hands and feet and kick her out of a fast moving vehicle in front of the gates of Langley."

"We can't do that," I said.

"Why not?" Zach asked, like he was seriously considering the idea.

"Because the enemy of my enemy is my friend." I started for the small room where we'd tied Catherine up the night before, but Zach lunged in front of me, blocking my way.

"I can't let you question her, Gallagher Girl," he told me.

"Isn't that why she's here—to talk?" I asked.

Zach shook his head. "She's here to *lie*."

"She'll talk to me."

"No, Cam," Zach said. "It's not a good idea."

"Maybe it's our only idea," I said back.

"Well . . ." I heard a tiny voice behind me and turned to see Liz standing there, a truly guilty look on her face. "Maybe not our *only* idea . . ."

Catherine sat in her chair, hands and feet bound, yet she looked like she was waiting on a train, like she'd wait forever if she had to.

"Hello, Catherine," I said, easing closer. She was across the room, but like a snake, I could feel her coiled, constantly ready to strike.

"You don't have to do this, Cammie," Zach said.

"Hello, darling," Catherine told him, but it was as if she'd never spoken at all.

"Gallagher Girl," he started again, but I couldn't take my eyes off of his mother.

"Liz," I said, and then my smallest roommate walked forward. She didn't tremble or shake, but I knew she must have been terrified as she pulled up the sleeve of Catherine's shirt and injected a clear liquid into the woman's arm.

"Truth serum, girls?" Catherine said. She sounded so disappointed. "Isn't that a tad cliché?"

"It's stronger," Liz said, then stepped quickly back. Zach moved between Liz and his mother until Liz was safely out of range of the woman tied to the chair.

"Really?" Catherine asked as Liz's concoction entered her bloodstream. It was like she was growing drunk and sleepy. Her eyelids were heavy, and when she told Zach, "You've gotten so tall," her words were slurred.

"Why are you hunting down the leaders of the Circle?" I asked, and Catherine looked at me for a long time, the tiniest of smiles playing at the corners of her mouth.

"It's good to see you, Cammie, dear. It's been too long."

"Are you sure we shouldn't hit her again?" Bex said from over my shoulder. "Because I totally think we should hit her."

I crouched on the floor, looked her in the eye. "You can talk to me, Catherine. Or you can talk to the CIA. Maybe the moles the Circle leaders have within the agency won't find you. But maybe they will."

"They're all dead, you know. The leaders. We just have one left."

"We?" I asked.

"Your mother and Joseph and I," Catherine said.

"She's lying," Zach said. "Joe would never work with her."

"Oh. Of course he would," Catherine told him. "He'd never admit it, but we want the same thing. We've always wanted the same thing. We just have different . . . *methods*."

"Like torture," I said.

Catherine looked right at me. "I didn't want to hurt you, Cammie. I really didn't. But it was the only way. I had to stop them, don't you know? I had to stop this. You had to help me. And you did help me. And now we're down to one. . . . Gideon Maxwell had one son and no grandchildren. His line stops there. There were no other heirs. So it's possible that there is no Maxwell descendant in the Circle now. Maybe there are just six Inner Circle members instead of seven. Maybe we're finished. But I doubt it. It doesn't *feel* finished."

Catherine seemed to think on that for a moment, and I had to admit that I agreed. Something in my bones told me it was still a long way from over.

"Maybe Maxwell appointed someone else to take his place before he died. But I honestly don't know." Catherine's gaze shifted onto Preston. "Why don't you ask him?"

Her hands were bound, and still Preston flinched, almost like he'd been slapped. I expected Macey to lash out at Catherine, but instead she turned to the boy beside her.

"Pres?" she asked. "Do you know?"

"No!" Preston's voice cracked and he shook his head. "I've never heard of Gordon Maxwell."

"Gideon Maxwell," Liz corrected.

"I don't know him! I don't know any of my dad's friends. Or . . . I don't know which of his friends might be in the Inner Circle." Preston seemed sad when he said it, as if he too had been living a lie. It was just that no one had bothered to tell him. "I don't know anything."

"Why are you doing this?" I turned back to Catherine. "Why did you betray the Circle's leadership?"

"I'm in the betrayal business." Catherine laughed. "Besides, I like the world the way it is. A world war is a highly inconvenient thing. I prefer my destruction on a much smaller scale."

"What do they want? What are the Circle leaders planning?" I asked.

"You know what they're planning," Catherine countered. She sounded almost bored, like we were wasting her time. She looked around Zach, to where Liz stood. "It was *her* plan, after all."

Liz shuddered but didn't speak or cringe or cry. I couldn't shake the feeling that our little roommate was growing up. We all were.

"Who is the mole at the Gallagher Academy?" I asked, but Catherine only looked at me as if I were crazy. "How did the Circle get Liz's test?"

"Oh, that." She shrugged. "The school has to file all of its admittance tests with the CIA. From there, it was easy enough for the Circle to acquire them just to see if there were any students we wanted to recruit . . ." She looked at Liz. "Evil plans we wanted to steal."

"Why?" Zach asked. "World war . . . what's in it for them?" He leaned down to his mother's level. "What do they want?"

Then Catherine looked at her son as if he were the most naive boy in the world. "They want *everything*," she said, and then she cackled. She was insane—there was no denying it. But she was also oddly lucid as she said, "The government is so big—so powerful. Cavan wanted the Union to fail—that's why he tried to kill Lincoln. It's the same agenda. They want what they've always wanted. Chaos. Fracture. Pieces so disorganized that no single player can ever have too much power." Then she laughed. "Of course, what they really mean but never say is that they don't want anyone to have more power *than they have*. Personally, I like power. It's one of many reasons I want to see them fail."

"Tell me what they're planning," Zach said.

"You know what they're planning," she countered. She was staring at Liz. "Don't you, Liz?"

"They want war," Liz said, her voice surprisingly strong.

"But is there war?" Catherine asked.

No. The answer swept over us all. *Not yet.*

"King Najeeb was a charismatic leader, but he was a grown man in a dangerous business. He still had enemies. His death, while sad, was not that tragic in the bigger scheme of things. And besides . . . it's not like he doesn't have *an heir*."

"The princess," I said, and Catherine nodded.

"A grown man blown to bits is sad. A small girl killed just days after her father. . . . An entire line wiped out. . . . That will cause the world to burn. The Iranians will have to break the treaty. And when the Iranians invade Caspia, Turkey will invade, and . . . boom."

"We have to find her," I said, turning to Zach.

"No." Catherine shook her head slowly. I don't know if Liz's drugs were finally becoming too much, but her voice had a hazy quality as she looked at me. "No. You don't."

"But we . . ." I started, then something in her eyes made me stop. She shook her head.

"You know where she is, Gallagher Girl." The words sounded different when Zach's mother said them. Haunting and dangerous and cruel.

"Amirah." I whispered the princess's name and thought about my first night back at school, about the tiny seventh grader with the big brown eyes and utterly royal countenance. "Amy. She goes to the Gallagher Academy, doesn't she?"

A dreamy smile spread across Catherine's lips. "Good girl," she told me. "It is a school fit for a queen. Now, go. Stop them."

"Step away from the psychopath!"

I knew the voice as soon as I heard it, but still part of me was almost afraid to turn around.

My aunt Abby's eyes were on fire, and she crossed the room in two long strides, grabbing my arm and physically pulling me farther from Zach's mother.

"Abby!"

At first, I was terrified—afraid my friends and I had been caught playing hooky. But then my fear turned to relief as I realized Abby and Townsend had found us. We didn't have to be on our own anymore.

"Abby, you're here! How did you find us? Did you get my messages? Were you—"

"We weren't following you," Townsend told us. "We were following *her*." He pointed to the woman tied to the chair, eyelids fluttering.

Finally, Abby released me and moved to examine Catherine.

"What did you do to her?" Abby asked. She picked up the empty syringe, smelled it. "Is that truth serum?" she asked, but Townsend just shook his head.

I could tell he was thinking about his own experience with that particular concoction when he huffed and said, "It's stronger."

"Well, isn't this precious?" Catherine smiled weakly and forced her eyes open, almost like she didn't dare drift off in the middle of the party.

"Abby, Catherine says the Circle is going to target Princess Amirah next," Bex said.

"Yes," Zach's mother said with a decisive nod. Then, just as quickly, she shrugged. "I think so. No one knows exactly what the Circle leaders will do. They are capable of anything, after all. But I believe that is their next move. So I came here to tell the good guys so that they can save the day. Isn't that what you do, darling?"

"Shut up! Just shut up!" Zach snapped. "I will never believe anything you say."

She looked at him and shook her head, smiled a little as she told him, "You are so like your father."

Then she looked past me and Zach, past Bex and Abby, to where Agent Townsend stood by the door with his arms crossed.

"What do you think, Townsend, darling? Isn't he like you?" She looked at Zach again. "I think he's just like you."

And then she closed her eyes and drifted off to sleep.

Chapter THiRtY-tHReE

Things my aunt said: *She lies.*

Things my boyfriend said: *She lies.*

Things my gut said: *She lies.*

Things I couldn't deny: *She was under the influence of truth serum.*

Things we all had to admit: *She wasn't lying.*

"Zach?" I asked, my voice too quiet in the darkness. The wind was strong and I could hear the waves crashing on the beach. Another storm was blowing in. I could feel it in the air. And as I stepped off the creaking porch and across the yard I tried again. "Zach." But he didn't answer.

I saw a dark shadow moving against the waves, leaning into the wind, so I walked down the tiny path, careful not to trip any of the alarms that had been set inside of him. I rubbed my arms and wished I'd brought a sweater, but Zach just stood in the blowing mist, his gray T-shirt growing steadily darker in the damp.

"Townsend is looking for you."

Zach laughed, a cold, cruel sound. "Well, eighteen years, folks. Glad he finally got around to it."

"Zach, he didn't—"

"Did *you* know?" he asked but didn't turn to face me.

"No, Zach. Of course not. Why would I know that?"

"Did Joe say anything to you? Did your mom?"

"My mom didn't know, Zach," I told him. "No one knew."

I thought about how Zach and Townsend had always reminded me of each other. They had the same posture, the same grin, the same earnest, serious nature. And now I knew why. I wished I'd seen it before then, and I also wished we could go back in time to before we knew. But we couldn't do either.

"She never told me!" Townsend's voice echoed from inside. Abby slammed a door, and the whole house shook.

"Has Abby killed him yet?" Zach asked.

I shook my head. "She'll get over it."

Then he turned to me, the moonlight slicing across his face. The wetness in the air grew heavier and water clung to his hair as he said, "Maybe I won't."

"Zach—"

"He left me. With her."

"He didn't know about you, Zach."

"He should have known! He's a spy. An operative. It was his job to know."

I eased forward, reached out to touch his arm.

"You should go talk to him, Zach. He's a good guy," I told him. "*You're* a good guy."

But Zach just shook his head. He looked like the saddest boy in the world when he told me, "I'm never having kids."

Let's get one thing straight. I'm eighteen years old as I write this. Kids? Totally not on my radar. In that moment, living through the next week was pretty much my only goal. But I can't say that Zach's words didn't stop me. That a part of my brain—the part that was trained to see fifty steps ahead—had to wonder what it meant. For me. For us.

"You aren't?"

"I wouldn't do that to a child."

"You'd be a good dad."

But Zach just laughed. It was a cruel, mocking sound. "Because I had such good parental role models?"

"You had Joe."

Then Zach turned back to the water and the darkness and the crashing, breaking waves. "I didn't have anyone."

I could have said, *You have me.* I could have taken his hand and told him everything was going to be okay—that there was no way the past would repeat itself. Not with us. But I learned a long time ago not to make those kinds of promises. I knew better than anyone that life can change on a dime. That even the best dads sometimes go away forever.

So instead I just asked, "What are we going to do about Amirah?"

"Who?" he asked, like he hadn't heard his mother at all.

"The princess, Zach. She's just a little girl. And that little girl is going to die. They're going to kill her."

Zach sank down to sit on a rock. He kept his gaze locked on the sea as he told me, "No, they aren't. We're not going to let them hurt anyone ever again."

Chapter THiRtY-fOUR

"Cam." I felt a kick against my leg. A bright light burned my eyes.

"Get up," Abby snapped. She stood above me, sunshine from the window spilling across her shoulders.

"What . . . what time is it?"

"Showtime."

I pulled my tennis shoes on over bare feet and raced after her down the creaky stairs.

"Where?" I asked, taking a few steps more. "Where are we going?"

Abby smiled. "Home."

You don't really appreciate things until they're gone. I know it's a cliché, but it's also true. I'd always known that someday I would leave the Gallagher Academy. We were just months from graduation when my friends and I decided to flee, after all. But even then I didn't realize how much I'd miss falling asleep in the common room with my classmates, some chick flick playing on the TV. I didn't know how much I'd miss my classes and my teachers—even homework would have been a welcome change from my new reality. (And don't even get me started on our chef's awesome crème brûlée.)

But most of all, I missed the building and the grounds. Some people say the Gallagher Mansion is a house. Some say it's a school. But for me, in that moment, all that really mattered was that it was my home. And I was coming back to it. But as excited as I was, that didn't mean I wasn't nervous.

"Are you sure this is a good idea?" Bex asked. It wasn't the first time that I had to wonder if she and I might share a brain. "I mean, I'm pretty sure fugitives from justice aren't supposed to go home."

"We're not going to stay long, girls," my aunt told us. "We're going to lock *that woman* in the Sublevels." Abby choked on the words. She refused to utter Catherine's name. "And then we're going to pick up Amirah and get her out of there. After that, we hit the road and lay low until this is over. Deal?"

"Deal," we all said in unison, and I couldn't resist turning around to eye the car that followed us.

Abby had insisted we split up—boys in Townsend's car, girls in the van. Maybe she had wanted to give Townsend a chance to bond with Zach. Or maybe she just couldn't stand the idea of being in the same vehicle as Catherine. (Even if Catherine was locked in the trunk.)

"Abby," Macey said carefully, "where will Amirah go?"

"Someplace safe, girls."

"But can't she stay here?" Liz asked. "The school is one of the most secure buildings in the country."

"Not until we know your mom and Joe have taken out the last member of the Inner Circle. Even then, she's still the queen of Caspia. She will need protection for the rest of her life. So the best thing for now is to take her someplace where no one will find her."

Of course my aunt was right. It was what we had to do. But I thought back to the girl I'd met the first night of the semester. She seemed so young and happy in our halls. I hated that we had to take her away from her school and from her friends. I hated that she was having to grow up so quickly. Largely, I guess, because I totally knew the feeling.

"Patricia!" Aunt Abby yelled, throwing open the front doors. "Dr. Fibs! Madame Dabney, we're back!"

It wasn't a terribly covert entrance, but I wasn't complaining when I saw Madame Dabney appear at the top of the stairs.

"Abby, it's so good to see you, darling!" She rushed toward us, pulled my aunt into a hug, then turned her gaze past Abby, to my roommates and me. Maybe it was the sun playing tricks on me, but I could have sworn I saw a tear roll down her cheek. "Welcome home, girls."

When I turned to the Grand Hall, I saw Professor

242

Buckingham standing in the doorway, frozen. It was like she didn't want to move—to break up the scene before her.

"Thank God you're safe."

But then everything in Buckingham's countenance shifted. She bristled and stood up straighter. I could have sworn she actually grimaced as Townsend and Zach dragged Catherine through the front doors. But she didn't flinch at the sight of the woman, not even when Catherine smiled in Buckingham's direction.

"Why, hello, Patricia." Catherine's gaze moved easily around the foyer and up the stairs. She wore shackles on her hands and feet and yet she examined the mansion as if she had more right to be there than Gilly herself.

"It is *so good* to be home," Catherine said, and I had a terrible feeling that Catherine hadn't lost—we hadn't captured her. That she was somehow exactly where she had always wanted to be.

"Shut up!" Zach snapped, and jerked on his mother's chains.

"Zachary," Buckingham warned. "Take her to Sublevel Two." Then Buckingham turned her gaze to Catherine. "We have a room all ready for you."

As soon as Catherine was gone, I expected the mood to lighten, the tension to ease. But it wasn't just Catherine's presence that had everyone on edge. It went far deeper than the awkward silence that coursed between Zach and Townsend. Something was wrong, and I felt it.

"What is it?" I asked, inching forward. "What's wrong? Is it my mom?"

"Your mother is fine, Cameron," Buckingham told me. "In fact, she and Joseph are very close to tracking down the Maxwell heir, if I'm not mistaken."

But something was wrong, and I wasn't going to stop until they told me.

"Then what's going on? Is it Amirah? Is she okay?"

"That's an interesting question, Cameron," Buckingham admitted. "To be perfectly honest, I don't know."

She didn't waver or try to skew the facts in her favor. The truth matters—every spy knows that much. And we needed the whole truth right then.

"Last night after we spoke, we sat Amirah down and told her everything you'd said about her father and the Circle." She looked at Abby then shook her head as if trying to cast aside her own doubts. "Maybe we should have waited. Her father just died. She's had so much change and pressure and—"

"What's wrong?" I asked.

"Well, it seems we cannot find her." Buckingham stood a little straighter. "It seems that Amirah has disappeared."

I know this much is true: Bex was right. It is a whole lot easier being the runner than the one left behind.

There were searches of the grounds and of the mansion. My friends and I spread out and covered every secret passageway a seventh grader could have conceivably found in one year. We interviewed her friends and reviewed the security footage. And when that all failed, we walked through the halls and across the grounds calling out her name. But Amirah never answered.

Finally, I found myself sitting on my bed. In our room. It was almost like we'd never left, and yet, at the same time, it was like we'd been gone for years. Books sat exactly where we'd left them among unfinished papers and study guides for untaken tests. It felt like I'd entered some kind of archeological dig site—the dorm rooms of Pompeii, a fleeting glimpse of our lives before the fire.

"We can't stay," Bex said.

"I know."

"The CIA may already know we're back—they could be sending a grab team for Preston and Zach, and maybe even you, right now."

"I know. But we can't leave her, Bex."

"Think, Cammie," Bex ordered. She grabbed me by the shoulders, made me face her. "Where is she?"

"How am I supposed to know where she is?"

"No." Liz shook her head. "Don't you see, Cam? You don't have to know where she is. You're supposed to know how she *feels.*"

Yeah. It's true. My friends are geniuses. And I was kind of foolish not to have seen it until then.

I turned and looked out the window, at our sweeping grounds and tall fences that more than ever before needed to keep one of us safe. And, beyond that, I saw the black stretch of Highway 10 and the lights of Roseville—the other world that existed just outside our reach.

"Normal," I whispered. "She's just learned she's never going to be normal."

"Amy?" I asked, but she didn't turn. It was almost like she'd forgotten the name she'd used at school. Her American nickname. Her code name. Her legend.

The tiny girl with the gleaming black hair just stayed seated in the little gazebo in the Roseville town square. As dusk settled around us, the white lights of the square began to glow. It looked like a movie set. A dream. And I remembered why, once upon a time, I had come there, looking for another life. It was why, when my friends and I had divvied up all the potential places where Amirah might have run, I chose that familiar square. It was as good a place as any to play pretend.

"You're back," Amirah told me when I joined her on the bench.

"Yeah," I said. "I guess I am."

"That's good." Her legs were so short she could swing them where she sat and they didn't scrape the ground. "We missed you. Tina Walters had a pool going on how long you'd be gone. I bet ten dollars that you'd show up at graduation in a helicopter."

"I could stay away a little longer if you'd like."

"No." Amirah shook her head. "I'm glad you're back now."

Prior to that moment I'd had one conversation with her. Just one. That was all. But it's true what they say about our sisterhood. It bonds us, forges us together. And with one look in that girl's eyes I knew that we were more bonded than most.

"I'm sorry about your father, Amirah. I tried . . ." I started, but my voice broke. I couldn't tell her that I'd been there. That I'd failed. I didn't think I could stand the idea of her hating me as much as I hated myself. "I believe he was a great man."

"He was." She held her head a little higher. She didn't face me as she wiped her eyes. "He had a duty. A legacy."

She almost grimaced with the word, and I knew that, like me, Amirah had been born into a most unusual family business.

"His father was hanged in the streets that surrounded our palace. My father was blown up outside the United Nations. But me . . . I was born in America. Am I an American, Cammie?" She faced me then. "Can I just be an American? Why do these people want to kill me for the sake of a country I've never even seen?"

"These people . . ." I stopped and considered my words. "These people don't care about you or your country. They just want governments to fall and chaos to rule. They think . . . they think the world is like a self-cleaning oven and they see you as the best way to turn up the heat."

Just like I had been the best way to track down a list.

It was clear to me in that moment that everyone was wrong about Amirah. She wasn't just a princess. She wasn't just a Gallagher Girl. She was me, at the beginning. She was a girl who had stumbled into something so much larger than herself that she couldn't possibly carry the weight alone.

"We should get you back to school, Amy. It's not—"

"Safe. I know." But she stayed seated, legs swinging in the glow of the Roseville town square twinkle lights. "I'm not safe."

"Maybe not right now. But you will be soon. My mother and Mr. Solomon . . . they are tracking down the people who want to hurt you. And they're getting close, Amy. I think they're really, really close. And when they're finished . . . then everything will be okay."

"No, Cammie. When these people are dead there will be others. There will always be people who want to hurt the queen of Caspia," Amirah said, even though, right then, she didn't look like a queen. She looked like a twelve-year-old girl who didn't want to go home and start her homework. And I, for one, totally couldn't blame her.

"You see that pharmacy?" I pointed to the far side of the square, the old-fashioned sign. "Abrams and Son," I said with a smile. "I used to date the son."

"Really?" the girl asked, and smiled wide. She might have giggled.

"Yeah. Sophomore year. It was a big scandal." I thought about Josh. He had been a dream once—a perfectly lovely piece of normal. But that dream was over.

"What happened?" she asked, like she already knew how the story was going to end. And she probably did. She was a Gallagher Girl, after all.

"I don't know exactly," I admitted. "We were really different, I guess. And then I met Zach, and a bunch of terrorists started trying to kidnap me, and I got too busy for a boyfriend."

"Come now, Cammie," Dr. Steve said with a chuckle. "Is that any way to talk to an old friend?"

"I already have enough friends, thanks."

"Where is she?" he demanded. "Where's Catherine?"

"The school. She's being held in one of the Sublevels."

He knew to stay back a little, far enough away that I couldn't kick or punch or wrestle the gun from his hands.

"Then we'd better start walking."

"Let Amirah go, Dr. Steve. You don't need her," I told him.

He laughed. "*They* need her, Cammie."

"I thought we were on the same side now," I tried to tell him. "Catherine said you just wanted to stop the Circle leaders and their war. To do that, we have to keep Amirah safe. We have to—"

"I don't *have* to do anything, Cammie!" He was shouting. It was like the rage and stress were too much for him, and he wanted it to end as much as I did. But then he stopped. There was a new light in his eyes—a realization that he had the power to change everything.

"The Inner Circle needs you to die," he said. His gaze fell on the girl behind me.

"That's why we have to get her back to school, Dr. Steve," I tried to tell him.

"They're going to assassinate you," he said to Amirah, but she didn't wince or speak. She just put her hand at the small of my back as I moved to shield her more.

"Yeah, but we're not going to let that happen, are we,

They were all good reasons—any one of them would do. But it wasn't the whole truth, and I knew it.

"I guess we just had different destinies. And I got tired of trying to outrun mine."

Amirah nodded slowly, but didn't say a thing.

"Come on," I told her. "You're not safe here."

She looked down at her hands. Sparkly pink nail polish chipping away. "I'm not safe anywhere."

And right then I wanted to cry. I wanted to hold her and smooth her hair and tell her everything was going to be okay. I wanted to say all the lies that, for months—for years—I had wanted to hear. And more than anything I wanted to believe that they were true. I wanted to tell her that I was okay—that I was proof that things get better and she wouldn't feel that way forever.

But before I could say a word she turned her big brown eyes to me and asked, "Are you okay, Cammie?"

I'd been chased, tortured, kidnapped, and almost killed, but I'd survived it. And I knew in my gut that if I could survive spy school, I could survive anything.

"I will be."

I took Amirah's hands and pulled her to her feet. She giggled a little, the sound light and free, dancing in the twinkling lights. I looped my arm through hers, and together we started across the square, toward Highway 10 and my third-favorite secret passage.

I was walking away from Roseville and sneaking back into

school for what might have been the last time, and so I stopped. Nostalgia took hold of me and turned me back to the pharmacy and the gazebo and the square.

And that was when I saw him.

"Hello, Cammie." Dr. Steve raised the gun in his hand, kept it trained in our direction. "I see you found our girl. Now, why don't you take me to Catherine?"

Chapter thiRtY-fivE

It's sad how accustomed a girl can get to having a gun p at her. I didn't tremble. I wasn't afraid. There were to other emotions coursing through me as I stood lookir man who had played with my mind for months and t me to a rooftop to die.

I felt the blood flow out of my face. My hands t heart pounded. And I thought for just one second sick. There was too much emotion inside of me, ar bile in my gut come to a simmer and then a boil, a to explode.

"Cammie?" Amirah's voice cut through the is that?"

"He's no one, Amy," I said, pushing her be someone I used to know."

"He looks familiar," she said.

"Don't look at him," I warned. "Don't tal not listen to him."

Dr. Steve?" I took a slow step forward, closing the space between us.

"No. They can't kill her if she's already dead."

He raised the gun higher, aiming it over my shoulder, and I knew there were no words—no logic—that could change what he was thinking. So *I* stopped thinking. I stopped waiting. I stopped planning and fearing and hating the man with the gun. I stopped being afraid for me, and I started caring only about my sister.

Without a word, I lunged in Dr. Steve's direction, faster than I ever knew I could move. It must have scared him because he fired. Once. Twice.

Blinding pain coursed through me, but I didn't stop. I just kept running toward him, catching his gun hand in my arms and spinning.

Was it starting to rain or was I sweating? I didn't know. All I was sure of was that a pair of headlights had appeared in the dark. The car was racing toward us.

Dr. Steve fired again, and I kicked, knocking him to his knees. The gun clattered to the ground and I spun, sending him into the street, right into the path of the speeding car.

I heard the crash.

I saw the blood.

And then there was nothing but the sight of Dr. Steve's crumpled body and the sound of Agent Edwards saying, "Cammie? Is that you?"

* * *

I don't know what I must have looked like, between the blood and the falling rain. My hair matted to my head and clung to my face, water dripping into my eyes as I squinted against the glare of the headlights. The windshield wipers of the car sloshed back and forth like a metronome.

"Cammie, you've been shot!" Agent Edwards looked from Amirah to Dr. Steve, lying bloody and broken on the ground. "Is he dead?"

"I . . . I don't know," I told him. Amirah was rushing toward me, terror in her eyes.

I watched Agent Edwards study her, almost as if she were a painting. "Amirah . . . it's you. You're safe. Thank goodness. Now, come on, you two. We've got to get you out of here."

He threw open the back door of the car, but for some reason I couldn't bring myself to go to him. Instead, I stooped to pick up Dr. Steve's gun. It was heavy and cold in my hands.

"Cammie, you're bleeding. Come on. We've got to get you girls back to school." He looked up and down the dark streets like he was worried about who or what might be coming for us next. "Cammie, come on."

My left arm felt useless at my side, but it didn't hurt, and I didn't move to get into the car. I couldn't. So instead I just asked, "What are you doing here, Agent Edwards?" I shifted a little, putting Amirah at my back.

"Cammie, I'm scared," she told me, but I kept my sights on the man in front of me.

"Ms. Morgan, come with me. Now!"

"Why did I wake up early?" I asked him. He looked at me as if I were as crazy as advertised. The girl who had been brainwashed, kidnapped. Broken. "In Alaska, I was supposed to sleep longer. And yet you came out early to check on me anyway. Was it an accident?"

"What are you talking about, Cammie? You're in shock. We don't have time for this."

"Did you want me to wake up early? Did you want me in that room when Ambassador Winters died?" He was frozen as I spoke. "Did you want me to die too?"

"Don't be ridiculous."

"There's something that's been bothering me all these weeks. Why did the CIA want Zach? Want me? We're just kids."

"Oh"—he laughed—"I think we both know you're more than that."

"The CIA had no reason to chase Zach and me . . . and Liz. *But the Circle did.*"

"Cammie, you and Amirah need to come with me. Now."

"Don't go with him, Amirah."

"I won't," she said. Her voice didn't tremble or break. She wasn't just a queen; she was a Gallagher Girl, as she told me, "I have your back."

I raised Dr. Steve's gun, took aim at the center of Agent Edwards's chest.

"You don't want to do that, Cammie," he told me.

"Yeah," I said, my voice even. "I think I do."

But the man in my sights just smiled and laughed.

"How long have you known?" he asked.

"Deep down . . . I think always. But for sure since the night of the career fair. You shouldn't have come for Zach and me. That was a mistake."

"No." He laughed then. "That was perfect."

I was just starting to ponder what he'd said—what it meant—when I heard a sniper's shots ring out.

"Down!" I yelled, pushing Amirah behind the car just as the windshield shattered.

Dr. Steve was right. The Inner Circle wanted Amirah to die, but she needed to die on their terms, and the more public her death the better. Something tragic. Something visible. So I was certain of one thing: Their sniper wasn't shooting at her. He was shooting at me.

I turned and, with my good arm, fired in the direction where the sniper must have been.

With my back turned, Agent Edwards didn't hesitate. He ran for Amirah, who ducked beneath his grasp and swept at his legs just like we all learned to do during Intro to Protection and Enforcement, but no seventh grader can take down a fully-trained operative, and when Amirah appeared again, Agent Edwards's arm was around her throat.

"Drop it, Cammie," he yelled, backing away, dragging Amirah with him. His gun was pressed against her temple. She trembled but didn't cry.

"Now!" he yelled. "I'll shoot her here. I will. I don't want to—there are so many more interesting ways for her to die. But she'll be dead either way, so it's your call. Now drop it."

Slowly I let Dr. Steve's gun fall to the ground.

The pain in my left arm was growing sharper and the rain fell harder. I knew that if Amirah and I didn't make it back to school soon, my friends would come looking for me. But I also knew that they would be too late.

"You don't have to die here, Cammie," he told me.

"Maybe I do," I said, and realized that I meant it. I would die to save Amirah. I would die to stop World War III.

"Cammie?" Amirah's voice broke, but she smiled. "Do you trust me?"

"Of course I do," I said, and then Amirah grabbed Agent Edwards's arm. And bit.

I killed a man once. I wasn't sure how the rifle got into my hands. I didn't remember firing. I didn't know what I was doing—how. Why.

This wasn't like that.

That night I was aware of everything. Every drop of rain. Every swipe of the wiper blades.

I knew exactly how long it took for me to fall to the ground and exactly where I'd find the gun. I remember the feel of the metal against my fingers. I was aware of my breath going in and out. And when Agent Edwards fired at me I was aware of that too.

Pain seared through me again—a hot, burning stab in my gut—and yet my body found a strength I didn't know it had, correcting as I fell. When I took aim at the very place Amirah had been just seconds before and pulled the trigger, I knew the risk. I knew the cost. And I would do it all over again in a heartbeat if I had to.

But I didn't have to.

Amirah's screams pierced the air, but she crawled away from the man who was falling to the ground. His blood was on her shirt, but she didn't seem to be in any pain. Her pain, I knew, would come later. For the moment at least, adrenaline and fear would keep her going, keep her safe.

"Cammie!" I heard my name ring out in the distance, but I was hearing things, I was certain.

Blood trailed into my eyes. Pain filled my body.

"Amirah," I said, grasping for her. "You have to get in the car. You have to drive it to the school. Go fast. Go now."

"I'm not going to leave you."

"I'll be okay," I told her. "I'll be—"

"*Cammie!*" I heard the voice again and that's when I grew certain I was dreaming, drifting slowly away.

"Just do me a favor," I said, the words barely louder than a whisper.

"Anything."

"Don't ever go anyplace without backup, okay?" I said, then laughed, but the pain was too much, and I crumbled over on the pavement. "It's a rookie mistake."

"Cammie, I can get you into the car," Amirah told me, but I just shook my head.

Someone had to stay with Dr. Steve. Someone had to watch Agent Edwards's body. There were a half dozen reasons I could have given for not getting into that car, but the truth was the one thing I didn't want to say: I didn't want Amirah to watch me die.

My eyes were too heavy then. The ground was so soft; I just wanted to lie there and sleep.

"Go, Amirah. Go and don't look back."

She nodded. Raindrops clung to her eyelashes, and when she blinked, I couldn't tell if she was crying.

"Cammie!" I heard my mother's voice again. I hadn't heard it in so long that it sounded like a ghost, calling to me, coming to take me to my father.

"Cammie," she said again and then she was there, holding me, pressing against my wounds. "Where are you hit, sweetheart? Where are you hit?"

"Mom!" I cried. "You came for me."

"No." My mother shook her head. I followed her gaze to the man on the ground. "We came for him."

"Is he . . ." I started, not quite able to bring myself to finish. Something was boiling up inside of me. It took a moment for me to realize that something was hope.

Mom smiled. "He's the final Circle leader, Cammie." My mother's breath came in ragged bursts, almost like she couldn't believe what she was saying.

"Final?" I asked. My voice broke.

"Maxwell Edwards was the great-great-great-great grandson of Gideon Maxwell."

"But I thought there were no Maxwell heirs," I said.

"He was illegitimate. That made him harder to track down. But we did it. We found him. He is the last one," Mom said. And I looked at the man on the pavement. He was supposed to look bigger somehow, more like a monster. But he was only a man. That's all any of them were—men and women. People whose anger affected their minds and poisoned everything they touched.

Mr. Solomon appeared. There was a gash at his temple and he carried a sniper rifle. Suddenly, I understood why Agent Edwards's backup had only gotten off one shot.

I watched my teacher kneel by the body and feel for a pulse.

"He's dead." Mr. Solomon stood and reached for my mother. "It's over."

"Joe, she's hit," Mom said, and I coughed again.

"You'll be fine, Ms. Morgan," Mr. Solomon said. "You're going to be fine, do you hear me?"

And I nodded my head, unwilling or just unable to disobey a direct order.

"Up," I said and forced myself upright.

"Sweetheart, the ambulance will be here soon," Mom told me.

"Dr. Steve," I said, and tried to stand.

"He's dead too." Mom pressed her scarf against my side, tried to stop the flow of blood. "Sweetheart, they're dead. They're gone. It's over."

And then I fell to the ground.

And cried.

Chapter thirty-six

Number of hours I was in surgery: 5

Number of hours I was unconscious: 9

Number of times I dreamed about the night before: 7

Number of times that, in that dream, I did things differently: 0

I woke to the sight of a dark figure standing at the window, watching.

"Zach?" I said and tried to move, but my left arm was too heavily bandaged.

"Sorry." Preston leaned into the light. "I'm afraid you're going to be disappointed."

He looked like the dorky boy who'd been standing in his father's shadow, on the verge of becoming the country's first son. He looked like the terrified kid who had jumped off a roof and had never heard the words *Circle of Cavan*.

"How do you feel?" he asked me. "Do you need the doctor or—"

"No." I shook my head. "I'm fine. I'm okay. Just . . . sit. Talk to me."

I watched him pull a chair closer to my bed, lean into the light of the blinking machines and hanging IV bags. He moved like someone who was afraid that I might break.

"How are you, Preston?" I asked. It was a question I'd been wondering for days, but there had never been a good time to ask it.

"I guess I'm great in comparison."

"Don't make me laugh," I told him.

He smiled. "Deal." Then he took my hand. "It's good to see you up. I was hoping you'd be awake before I had to go."

"You're leaving?" I asked.

He looked down at the bed, at my bruises and my bandages. "Yeah. I think it's probably for the best, you know. Your mom has been great. She offered to try to get me enrolled or whatever—finish out the school year here with all of you, but . . ." He trailed off. It seemed to take forever for him to look at me again, and when he did it was like I was seeing him for the very first time.

"Thank you for getting me out of that place, Cammie. Have I thanked you yet?"

"You don't have to say that," I told him, but Preston just shook his head.

"No. I really do. I might have died in there. It could have killed me," he said, and I knew he wasn't talking about his body. That place was a prison, but it was designed to kill your soul. "Anyway, now I think I have to leave." He stood slowly.

"No. You don't."

"Yeah." He smiled down and squeezed my hand. "I think it's time for me to go be with my family."

"Preston, wait!" I tried to sit up, to reach for him, but the movement was too much.

"You're in pain," he said. "Let me get the doctor to give you something."

"There's a button for the morphine, but I don't like it. It knocks me out."

"You know, it's okay to admit a little weakness now and then, Cammie. It won't kill you. In fact, I hear it makes you stronger."

"Cam!" Mom cried, and held her arms out wide. She acted like she was going to hug me, then thought better of it at the last minute. "How are you, kiddo?" she asked instead. Her hair was longer and, if possible, shinier. She had more color in her cheeks, like she'd been on a beach or a ski slope—maybe both. I'm not going to say she was glowing, except . . . well . . . she was totally glowing. She looked alive and at peace and . . . happy. My mother looked happy.

I hadn't realized until then the degree of sadness that had always loomed around her before. A subtle, constant hum that coursed through everything she said and did. But it was finally gone.

"How do you feel, sweetheart?"

She pushed my hair away from my face, and her voice was like a cool cloth on my forehead.

"Fine. I think."

I tried to sit up, but my mother pushed me back down.

"Easy, now. You had a close one."

"Am I . . ."

"You're going to be fine," my mother told me.

"Amirah?" I asked.

Mom smiled. "She's going to be fine too. She left this morning. We have a team of Gallagher Girls on her. She will be held in a secret location for the time being, but then . . . She'll be fine, Cammie. We'll keep her safe."

And only then did I really let myself believe it.

I watched my mom straighten. It was almost like flipping a switch as she transitioned from mother to headmistress.

"I'd say you dodged a bullet, but you didn't," she told me. "Still . . . you were lucky." She smoothed my hair again. "Dr. Steve shot you in the arm. The doctors expect you to regain full use of it with a little physical therapy. You get to wear that sling for a while, though."

"And the other bullet . . ." I tried.

"It could have been bad, Cam. It could have been really bad, but somehow Agent Edwards managed to miss all the major organs. You were lucky," she said again.

I shifted on the bed. Pain shot through me, and I winced. *Lucky* wasn't the word I would have used, but my mother was right. She usually is.

I heard her talking about security protocols and the chances of attack. Part of me listened to every word as she talked about what Zach's mom had said, the threat the little girl who called herself Amy was probably under at that very moment.

But another part of me—the girl part, not the spy part— just kept looking at the simple diamond ring on my mother's left ring finger.

"Mom . . ." I heard my voice crack.

"Hello, Ms. Morgan."

I turned and saw Mr. Solomon walking into the room. He looked like the most handsome man alive as he put his arm around my mother's waist and kissed her cheek.

"Well, kiddo." Mom blushed as she looked up at Mr. Solomon. "There's something we need to talk about."

I looked from my mother to my CoveOps teacher—my father's best friend. Once upon a time, he had sworn to take care of me and my mom should anything ever happen to my dad. And he'd done that. Joe Solomon loved me, I was sure of it. But he was *in love* with my mother. And part of me knew that he always had been.

"Ms. Morgan," Mr. Solomon started cautiously, "if you'll—"

"Yes," I blurted. Tears ran down my face. "Yes, I give you my blessing to marry my mother."

Things were supposed to return to normal after that, but they didn't.

Maybe it was because, once again, I was lying in a hospital bed. Maybe it was because we'd seen how fragile peace was, how delicate a line we walked. Maybe it was because we were seniors, and Liz had stopped worrying about the fate of the world and started worrying about college admissions. (Thus far, she'd been accepted at Harvard, Yale, Brown, Stanford, MIT, and six other schools she hadn't technically applied to.)

But my worries looked different than they had before.

"What do I call him? I mean, I can't exactly call him Mr. Solomon. Or do I? Do I call him Mr. Solomon? Or Joe?" I looked from Bex to Macey, who shrugged in response, and I talked on. "I mean, he's still my teacher. But he's also going to be my stepfather. Do stepfathers get called 'stepfather'?"

But then I saw Zach walking down the hall toward my room, and I couldn't finish. It felt wrong worrying about my new stepfather when his own paternal issues were still so totally up in the air.

"Hey," I said. "How are you?"

Liz moved from the end of my bed and Zach eased closer, carefully, like I was still entirely too fragile.

"I'm pretty sure I'm supposed to be asking *you* that." He leaned down and kissed the top of my head. "Remind me to kill you later for going off like that."

"It hurts when I laugh," I told him.

"Good. Because I'm not joking." He didn't smile, but he kissed me again, on the lips, and moved to the window, almost like he was standing guard. He looked like Agent Townsend, but I didn't say so.

There was a TV in my room, and the newscasters kept talking about how the riots in Caspia were dying down. The film crews that had surrounded the UN were gone. All that remained, it seemed, were two dead traitors in the streets of

Roseville and a bullet-riddled teenage girl. No one seemed to know how close we'd come to World War III—how it might have really happened if Catherine had never come in from the cold.

Catherine.

"Where is she, Zach?" I asked. "Where is your mom?"

"Mommy dearest is in Sublevel Two for the time being," Zach said. "There has been some debate about what to do with her. The CIA wants her, of course, but until all the moles are out of the agency, your mom and Joe don't want to let her out of their sight."

I couldn't blame them.

"What about you, Bex?" Liz asked.

"What about me?" Bex wanted to know.

"Well, if you go to Oxford, then maybe I'll consider going there too. What are you going to do after graduation?"

"MI6," Bex said with a confident nod. "I don't want to wait anymore. I want to get to work."

Liz looked at Macey.

"Secret Service," Macey said. She fingered the samples of fabric she was holding, looking down at them as if she couldn't face us while admitting her deepest, darkest secret. "I'm going to join the Secret Service. The president has a teenage daughter. And I can't help thinking that maybe I can do for her what Abby did for me."

Finally, Liz looked at me, but I didn't have an answer to her question.

On the TV, a reporter was outside the Capitol building,

talking about the days we'd just lived through. Iranian forces were moving away from the Caspian border. The unrest was almost over, and the Iranian ports would soon be reopened for business. The world at large knew that we had come close to tragedy, but would they ever know exactly how close? And wasn't that our job—to make sure they didn't have to?

"So does that mean it's over?" I asked, the words only for myself, but the smartest girls in the world were beside me, and in unison they turned to look at the screen.

"I guess," Liz said. She didn't sound hopeful, though. We'd all seen how tenuous the peace was. We knew too well how easily it could all be broken—how quickly it could all happen again. There would always be people who wanted war and power and dominance. They would always be there, but, luckily, so would we.

"Periwinkle or persimmon?" Macey asked. She held two scraps of fabric out for me to examine, but I was heavily drugged and more than a little skeptical.

"What are you talking about?" I asked.

"Bridesmaid dresses. Your mom said I could plan the wedding. She doesn't care, and between you and me I'm so relieved. It was going to be really hard to manipulate her into letting me make all the decisions anyway. So, periwinkle or persimmon?"

I pointed to one, and to tell you the truth I didn't care which one it was. That's the thing about getting shot twice, almost kidnapped twice, really kidnapped once, and banged on the head more times than anyone can imagine: it tends to put your priorities in order. And I didn't care what color my dress was as long as the members of the wedding were happy and healthy and . . . there.

As long as everyone I loved was there.

"Spring in the gardens," Macey said. Outside the windows, I could see the first sprinkles of green starting to cover the trees. The sun was shining and the sounds of laughing, running girls filled the halls. "After graduation."

She nodded as if that were our most important mission yet—maybe our final mission on those grounds, all of us together. In periwinkle gowns.

Chapter thirty-seven

"Hello, Cammie," Catherine said as she stood in the shadows.

Sublevel Two was empty. I'd walked without a sound down the spiraling stone walkway to the room that had become a cell. The door was gone, replaced with a massive clear barrier that was no doubt blast-proof and bulletproof, and the only way in or out of the room that had been Zach's mother's home for the rest of the semester. But the semester was ending. Graduation was coming.

It was time to say our good-byes.

"This is such a nice surprise," she told me. A harsh light burned overhead, casting her face in eerie shadow as she sat on the small mattress that lay on the floor. "But, of course, I knew you'd come eventually. I knew you had to come."

It was my turn to speak—to say something. I wanted to ask her where I had messed up the previous summer—exactly how and when and why I'd gotten caught. I might have begged her to tell me if betraying our sisterhood was worth it. I might have yelled and cursed and cried for all she'd done to me. To Zach. To us. I might have done any of those things, but I couldn't speak. So I stood, wordless, watching her, almost like looking at a dream.

"How do you like my room?"

She gestured to the stone walls and floor. There were big pads of paper and crayons, two blankets and a pillow without a case, but no chair and no window, just a bare lightbulb that swung overhead.

"Don't feel bad for me, Cammie," she told me. "I'm home, after all." She stretched out on the narrow mattress, looked up at the ceiling. "I always knew I'd come home."

I hated that fact, and she must have seen it in my eyes, because she straightened.

"What's the matter, Cammie? Did you forget that we are sisters?"

I couldn't speak. Words formed inside my mind, but I couldn't will my mouth to say them.

"How is Zachary? He hasn't come to see me. Will you ask him to come? I would consider it a personal favor."

I'm not doing you any favors.

"Your mother comes and sees me every day. She has lots of questions."

As she spoke, she looked like an insane person. Like she had a child's mind inside that fully grown body. I wondered if it was an act, but then I didn't care.

"Look, Cammie." She picked up one of the pieces of paper. "It's the mansion, see? It's our home." She unrolled the paper and held it toward the glass to reveal a drawing of the mansion made with crayons. "I made it for you." She rolled the paper up again and slid it through the narrow opening in the glass. I took it, but I didn't say a word.

"Doesn't our home look like a castle in my picture?" she asked me. "I always thought it looked like a castle."

And then she started to sing.

"Above the plains up on the hill there stood a castle bold
A gleaming palace made of white, a pillar to behold
The horsemen lived in service to the castle and the crown
But the knights rose up and killed the kings
And it all burned down."

"That song."

I hadn't realized I'd said the words aloud until Catherine's eyes widened.

"Do you recognize it, Cammie?" she asked. "Did I sing it to you last summer in Austria?"

Honestly, I didn't remember. Maybe she had. But that wasn't why I knew it.

"Oh," Catherine said, realization dawning. She pressed her fingers against the glass. "I sang it to Zachary. Tell me, dear, does he sing it to you now?"

I didn't answer. I just inched farther from the glass as if she might reach out, touch me with a spark.

"They are going to take me away tonight. Did you know that, Cammie? Did you know I'm leaving?"

I didn't tell her that I did know. I didn't say that that was why I had come—that I needed to close this final chapter. I wanted to see her there—frail and fleeting and locked inside those walls and the unhinged balance of her mind. I needed to see the woman from the roof in Boston, from the streets in D.C., from the nightmares of Austria that still invaded my mind. I needed to see her caged like an animal and know that it was over.

But I didn't say that. I didn't dare admit that she still had any power over me. I didn't give her that one little bit of satisfaction.

She looked up at the walls and the ceiling—the stone that surrounded her.

"They promised me that this would always be my home. That girls like you would always be my sisters. But they weren't my sisters, were they?" Catherine asked, but then the lunacy broke, a quick and fleeting crack, and through it I saw anger and bitterness and rage.

I saw the girl who had come to the Gallagher Academy looking for a home and found only a thing to hate. I saw the Catherine who had found, in the Circle, an outlet for her anger. I saw the woman who had tortured me once and who would gladly do it again.

"Why did you come to us, Catherine?" I asked her, finally. "You knew you would end up here—like this. Why did you do it?"

She smiled, but I guess it was her turn not to answer, to withhold a small sense of power. Instead, she just sat cross-legged on the cold stone floor and began to sing.

"But the knights rose up and killed the kings
And it all burned down."

Chapter thirty-eight

That night I woke up to the sound of sirens.

"Code Black. Code Black. Code Black."

Our graduation gowns hung on hangers from the bathroom door. A few of our things were already in boxes with labels like LIZ'S ROOM and MACEY STORAGE, but for the most part our suite looked exactly like it always did, books and clothes strewn everywhere, like in the homes of normal teenage girls.

Except we weren't normal.

That was obvious as soon as the sirens broke through the air. Macey was already out of bed and pulling on her shoes. Bex was at the window, staring out across the grounds, but then in the blink of an eye, the view disappeared. Titanium shutters descended, covering the windows and blocking off all chance of us getting out. Or of someone else getting in.

"Liz," Bex shouted. "Get up!"

"What's going on?" Liz asked, voice groggy.

"Catherine," I said, my blood going cold. "Tonight they're moving Catherine."

The halls were full as we made our way downstairs. The sirens boomed and the lights swirled, and I felt almost dizzy from the noise and the pressure. Protective cases covered all the archives, and I could hear the sounds of yelling, cries booming out through the chaos.

"Downstairs and into the Grand Hall please, ladies!" Mr. Smith yelled from the landing. "Down the stairs! Yes, please. Slowly, now. No need to rush. No need to panic. Into the Grand Hall!"

Calmly, my roommates and I fell into step with the tide of girls that was sweeping toward the Hall of History. It was organized chaos, with the swirling lights and meandering half-asleep crowds. It felt less like a drill and more like the zombie apocalypse.

"Gallagher Girl." Zach came rushing up behind me.

"What's going on?" Bex asked, and we stopped, stepping into the Hall of History and out of the parade of pajama-clad girls that still moved dutifully down the stairs.

"They were moving my mother when she got away." He seemed out of breath. "All the security staff and most of the teachers are out looking for her. They've locked down the mansion, but it's probably too late. She's probably already escaped."

"Yes, right this way!" Tina Walters was shouting from the base of the stairs. "Into the Grand Hall, munchkins. No. We're not going to open up the waffle bar," Tina told one over-anxious eighth grader. "Inside, now."

"Do they really think she's gone, Zach?" Liz asked, but I could see the answer in his eyes.

"I should have known it was too good to be true," Zach said. "She never would have turned herself in if she hadn't had a plan."

The words hit me so hard, I actually had to lean against the railing. I'd been thinking the same thing for weeks—ever since the day when Agent Townsend and Zach walked a shackled Catherine back into our school and she had looked around as if she was exactly where she wanted to be. I thought about the woman behind the glass, the empty look in her eyes, and the cold fury in her words. And finally the song that she had sung to me.

Zach was right. She'd always known we were going to bring her back to the Gallagher Academy. But he was wrong about one thing.

His mother never intended to leave.

"It all burned down," I sang.

Zach's eyes went wide. "Where did you hear that song?"

"I went to see your mom last night."

"You shouldn't have done that, Gallagher Girl. You should never have—"

"Zach, stop! Listen to me. She's not leaving." I gripped his T-shirt and made him look into my eyes. "She's going to burn the castle to the ground."

I waited for someone to tell me I was crazy, but then the

floors shook. For a moment, the sirens stopped. An eerie, hollow silence followed and no one moved.

"We have to evacuate the mansion," I said.

"It's going to be okay, Cam," Macey said. "I mean, the school has state-of-the-art fire protection mechanisms, right? Liz, right?"

But Liz didn't hurry to agree. She had her fingers against her lips again, calculating.

"Liz, what's wrong?" Bex asked.

"It's probably nothing," she blurted in a way that meant it was totally something.

"What?" I snapped again.

"It's just that Dr. Fibs and I have been working on a new kind of power source. We want to take the Gallagher Academy completely off-line in five years, and we think that this has tremendous green technology implications if—"

"Liz!" Bex snapped, bringing her back into focus.

"It's an energy source," Liz said again.

"And . . ." Macey prompted.

"That means it can also be a bomb."

Before any of us could process what that meant, smoke began to rise up the stairs, sweeping through the hallways and filling the Hall of History. The sirens came again, switching from Code Black to the shrill haunting sound of the fire alarms.

"Fire!" someone yelled from down below.

I watched the doors and windows, waiting for them to open, but the fire alarm must not have been able to override a Code Black, because they stayed barred, trapping us inside.

Panic was starting to grow. Girls rushed toward the doors. The windows. Yells turned to cries, screams that pierced the air. And the younger girls were pushing, going nowhere.

"Tina!" I yelled over the railing.

Down below she was struggling with the doors, trying to get them to open. Eva Alvarez and Courtney Bauer were trying to break the windows.

"They're locked!" Tina yelled just as the sprinkler system sprang to life. Water erupted from the ceiling, spraying down on us, drenching us, but no one could move to escape it.

"They're all locked!" Courtney yelled to me.

"Not all of them," I said.

I ran down the stairs and to the old bookcase I'd first discovered during the spring semester of my eighth grade year. If you pulled out a book called *Spymasters of the Ming Dynasty* while pushing on the bookcase's left-hand side, you could make the whole thing spin around, a revolving door into a dusty tunnel that spiraled down into the depths of the school and finally emerged just west of the guard tower on the north side of the grounds.

"In here!" I yelled and Tina rushed toward me. "Go down the corridor. Keep going. It will get you out of the mansion."

"Munchkins!" Tina shouted, her voice echoing over the cries of the screaming underclassmen, and, instantly, the foyer went silent. "Follow me!" Tina yelled, and the girls did exactly as they were told.

I found another passageway and opened it too, sent Courtney and Eva into that tunnel, doubling the flow of girls fleeing the mansion. And as the halls filled with smoke, they cleared of girls until only my friends and Zach and I were left.

"Cam!" Macey shouted. She was half in the tunnel already, looking back at me. "We have to go."

But I looked around the hallways. The smoke was so thick I could barely see, and yet I couldn't stand the thought of leaving.

"I have to find my mom! And Abby! And—"

"They're outside looking for my mom," Zach told me, but I couldn't believe him. I wanted to check her office—to go search her room.

"Gallagher Girl, we have to go. Now!"

In the Hall of History, there was a crash. A piece of the ceiling collapsed on one of the cases. Sparks rained down over the railing of the balcony like sparklers on the Fourth of July.

"Go," I said, pushing Liz and Bex toward the opening. "Go," I told Zach. "I'm right behind you."

I always used to joke that I could walk down the secret passages of the Gallagher Academy blindfolded. Well, that night I got to prove it. Darkness swallowed us. The smoke was so heavy in places that we had to pull our shirts up and cover our mouths. My eyes burned and watered, and the air was so dry it was like breathing sand.

Still, the air grew fresher with every step. The lower we got, the farther we moved from the fires. The passageway was leading to freedom—I could feel it. We just had to keep walking, moving, following the path.

But then I heard the singing.

I could see Bex and Zach up ahead with Liz and Macey. No one was behind me, I was sure. And I stopped just to listen—just to make sure—when I heard the voice again, louder now.

"It all burned down."

That passageway didn't branch, I was certain. There was nothing down there but old timbers and cobwebs. There was nothing, I was sure. Except the voice was there. I heard it.

"The knights rose up and killed the kings."

I backtracked and followed the sound of the voice until I reached a place where the passage widened. I'd never noticed it before and I might not have seen it then, had it not been for the smoke, the way it spiraled there, as if caught in a draft.

I turned to the wall, pushing and pressing until . . . *pop.* A door swung open, and there she was.

"Don't do this, Catherine," I told her.

Slowly the woman turned. Her hair was greasy and matted. Dirt and grime clung beneath her nails, and yet she smiled at me as if she were a contestant in a pageant.

"Hello, Cammie," she said.

She sounded so calm—but then I saw Liz's device in her hands.

"What are you doing with that?" I asked her.

"You know what I'm doing with it," she said. She pointed to the heavy beams that crisscrossed the ceiling. "Every structural support in the entire mansion can be traced to right here. Did you know that, Cammie?"

I shook my head. "No. I've never seen this room before." And I hadn't.

As secret rooms go, that one was massive. I was on something of a balcony, looking down on where Catherine stood below. A rickety staircase led toward her, and I studied the space. I think it might have been a cellar once, cold storage for the pre-refrigeration era. More tunnels spiraled out from where she stood, and I knew that one of them must have led to the lake, because there was a wetness in the air. It probably would have been cool there on a normal day, but with the fires raging above us, the dampness felt more like steam.

"How disappointing," Catherine said, and she sounded like she honestly meant it—like I wasn't quite the formidable opponent she had thought me to be. "This was always my favorite room."

Candles burned all around her. It was almost like a temple. A shrine. I could see her retreating to that place during her time at the Gallagher Academy, Catherine's favorite place for hiding. But I imagine that, unlike me, she never had friends who tried to find her.

"I used to spend so many hours down here. I used to love to get lost. But I don't have to tell you what that feels like, do I, Cammie? I can see why Zachy likes you. You know what they say, boys always fall for girls just like their mothers."

I wanted to tell her that she was crazy—that she was wrong. But Catherine and I had both retreated to those dark and secret places. We had pushed through the cobwebs and the shadows in search of the secrets of the past. Yeah. She was right. We had a lot in common. But I knew the kind of girl I wanted to be when I reached the end of the tunnel. I wanted to climb out into the light.

"Don't you think we're alike, Cammie?"

"No." I shook my head and, in that moment, I meant it. I really did. "I think you're angry. And hurt. And vengeful." I tried to take a deep breath but the smoke made me cough. "I think you're incredibly vengeful."

"Maybe I am." She looked up at me with a smirk. "But I'm the one with the bomb."

"You don't have to do this," I said. "You'll never make it out alive. If you set that off now, you'll die here."

"You still don't get it, do you? I won't die today. And I didn't die the day I left your precious school—your sisterhood. I died the day I came to it."

I don't understand hate. I've seen its power. I've known its wrath. I've even felt it coursing through my own veins, pushing me on. But I don't know where it comes from or why it lasts, how it can take hold in some people and grow.

I heard a cracking sound, like thunder. Sparks rained down, and I jerked back just as a beam crashed overhead, showering me with smoke and flames, and yet I wanted to run through the falling ash. Stop her once and for all.

"Gallagher Girl!" Zach grabbed my arm and jerked me around to face him. I hadn't even heard him come up behind me.

"Hello, Zachy," Catherine said from below, but Zach didn't even look at her.

"We've got to go," he said, starting to drag me away.

"Zach, we can stop her." I fought against him with all I had while, down below us, Catherine started singing once again.

"We can still save the school!" I yelled.

A hundred and fifty years of history stood around me. It was the place I loved. It was my home. My destiny. That building was in my veins, and without it, I feared that I might die.

"Zach, we have to stop her!"

But Zach just held me. He looked at me with shock and awe and just a little bit of wonder. In spite of everything, I thought that he might laugh.

"Gallagher Girl," he told me, "you *are* the school."

Then he held my head between his hands and kissed me, hard and fast, breaking whatever trance I was in.

"Zachy!" Catherine called from below.

"Good-bye, mother," he yelled over the railing. "I will never see you again."

Then Zach took my hand and together we ran into the passageway. Smoke swelled and I kept running, away from the fire and the woman, fleeing from the ghosts.

And when the blast came, it was like an earthquake, a tsunami of stone and timber and dust that we were trying to outrun.

The passageway crumbled behind us. The beams were rimmed with fire—red sparks shooting through the dry and decaying timbers, racing us toward the cool, clear air of the night.

I still remember seeing the Gallagher Academy for the first time. I'd just never realized I would someday see it for the last time.

"Zach . . ." I started, but the word caught. Was it smoke in my lungs—in my eyes? Because I was crying. I couldn't stop crying.

I could hear my mother's voice, yelling, "Cammie! Has anyone seen Cammie?"

"Mom! Mom, I'm here!"

Tears streaked down her face, mixing with the soot and the ash.

"Is everyone okay?" I asked. "Did everyone get out?"

"Yes." My mother hugged me. "Cammie, are you okay?"

And for the first time in two years I said, "Yes," and I absolutely meant it.

The fire grew. Flames swept upward, smoke spiraling toward the sky, but I just held tightly to my mother and watched the windows shatter, the floors collapse.

We stood for hours, watching as the fire raged and the sky brightened. I stood in the middle of a crowd of girls with soot-stained faces and bloody knees, living to spy another day.

Chapter Thirty-nine

"Courtney Elaine Bauer," Madame Dabney said.

Applause filled the stands. Someone whistled. And Courtney looked like an angel as she walked across the stage to take her diploma and shake my mother's hand.

"Rebecca Grace Baxter," Madame Dabney said, and this time Bex climbed onto the stage.

I glanced at her parents, who sat in the front row of folding chairs. Her dad had a video recorder out, documenting the entire thing. Her mother smiled and clapped and waved, and I remembered that for a truly exceptional school, graduation at the Gallagher Academy is pretty much like graduations everywhere. There are smiling parents and gushing girls, shapeless black gowns and new graduates standing on the verge of a brave new world.

The only difference is that our worlds are slightly braver than average.

One by one we crossed the stage and shook my mother's hand. Gilly's sword had been shielded in its protective case and had come through the fire without a scratch, and like all Gallagher graduates before us, we stopped and kissed its blade. We held our diplomas and moved our tassels and when my turn came I was frozen for a moment, looking back over the crowd.

There were Mr. Solomon and Zach and Agent Townsend, who held tightly to Aunt Abby's hand. My teachers smiled back at me. The underclassmen looked up at the senior class in awe. And I squinted against the sun, looking across the grounds at the scaffolding that rose in the distance. I saw the mansion growing, stretching up from the ashes. I saw our fresh start.

"And now a few words from our valedictorian, Ms. Elizabeth Sutton."

Liz looked especially short as she stood behind the podium. Macey had forced her to wear heels, and she shifted uncomfortably from foot to foot as she adjusted the microphone and started to speak.

"What is a Gallagher Girl?" Liz asked.

She looked nervously down at the papers in her hand even though I knew for a fact she had memorized every word.

"When I was eleven I thought I knew the answer to that question. That was when the recruiters came to see me. They showed me brochures and told me they were impressed by my test scores and asked if I was ready to be challenged. And I said yes. Because that was what a Gallagher Girl was to me then, a student at the toughest school in the world."

She took a deep breath and talked on.

"What is a Gallagher Girl?" Liz asked again. "When I was thirteen I thought I knew the answer to that question. That was when Dr. Fibs allowed me to start doing my own experiments in the lab. I could go anywhere—make anything. Do anything my mind could dream up. Because I was a Gallagher Girl. And, to me, that meant I was the future."

Liz took another deep breath.

"What is a Gallagher Girl?" This time, when Liz asked it, her voice cracked. "When I was seventeen I stood on a dark street in Washington, D.C., and watched one Gallagher Girl literally jump in front of a bullet to save the life of another. I saw a group of women gather around a girl whom they had never met, telling the world that if any harm was to come to their sister, it had to go through them first."

Liz straightened. She no longer had to look down at her paper as she said, "What is a Gallagher Girl? I'm eighteen now, and if I've learned anything, it's that I don't really know the answer to that question. Maybe she is destined to be our first international graduate and take her rightful place among Her Majesty's Secret Service with MI6."

I glanced to my right and, call me crazy, but I could have sworn Rebecca Baxter was crying.

"Maybe she is someone who chooses to give back, to serve her life protecting others just as someone once protected her."

Macey smirked, but didn't cry. I got the feeling that Macey McHenry might never cry again.

"Who knows?" Liz asked. "Maybe she's an undercover journalist." I glanced at Tina Walters. "An FBI agent." Eva Alvarez beamed. "A code breaker." Kim Lee smiled. "A queen." I thought of little Amirah and knew somehow that she'd be okay.

"Maybe she's even a college student." Liz looked right at me. "Or maybe she's so much more."

Then Liz went quiet for a moment. She too looked up at the place where the mansion used to stand.

"You know, there was a time when I thought that the Gallagher Academy was made of stone and wood, Grand Halls and high-tech labs. When I thought it was bulletproof, hack-proof, and . . . yes . . . fireproof. And I stand before you today happy for the reminder that none of those things are true. Yes, I really am. Because I know now that a Gallagher Girl is not someone who draws her power from that building. I know now with scientific certainty that it is the other way around."

A hushed awe descended over the already quiet crowd as she said this. Maybe it was the gravity of her words and what they meant, but for me personally, I like to think it was Gilly looking down, smiling at us all.

"What is a Gallagher Girl?" Liz asked one final time. "She's a genius, a scientist, a heroine, a spy. And now we are at the end of our time at school, and the one thing I know for certain is this: A Gallagher Girl is *whatever she wants to be*."

Thunderous, raucous applause filled the student section.

Liz smiled and wiped her eyes. She leaned close to the microphone.

"And, most of all, she is my sister."

Chapter forty

Six Months Later

Some girls are looking at me as I write this. Well, not *me*, exactly. I think they want this table. I can't really blame them. It's warm here in the sun with the cool breeze washing over these pages. Every now and then I reach down to smooth my plaid skirt, but then I remember that my plaid skirt days are behind me.

Some guys throw a Frisbee across the quad. A man in a tweed jacket parks an old-fashioned bicycle near the library. And I sit here, alone and unseen.

A chameleon.

Turns out, you can take the girl out of the spy school, but you can never take the spy school out of the girl.

"Here you go," I tell the guys and send the Frisbee back to them, harder than they must have expected.

"Hey, thanks," one of the guys tells me. "Wow. You're really strong."

He has no idea.

He's cute, Bex would say. But Bex isn't beside me. None of my friends are here, so I'm alone when the guy asks, "Have I seen you before?"

I gather my things and have to smile.

"Nope," I tell him.

"See you around?" the guy asks.

I doubt it.

He doesn't know my story. He hasn't seen my scars. To him, I'm just another freshman, another girl. He can't possibly understand why I blend so easily into the wave of backpacks that fills the sidewalk. He doesn't know me, and I realize that maybe I don't know myself. That I have a lifetime to figure that out.

People say Georgetown University is prettiest in spring, but the autumn air feels sweet to me. It's the closest thing to freedom that I have ever felt. When the path branches, I can either walk along the main road to and from campus or go down an overgrown path that runs along the river. Most coeds would be afraid to go down the dark, twisting trail alone, but I don't think twice about it. I walk on, sun streaking through the falling leaves until I pass beneath a stone archway.

Overhead, cars and pedestrians and cyclists make their way to campus. They don't think about what's down below, but I walk on without another thought.

When I find the derelict-looking door, I punch a code into a cleverly hidden box and turn the knob. Once inside the cold space, I don't blink as the red line sweeps across my eyes, reading my retinas. I hold my hand to the sensor and wait for another steel door to swing open. Then I step inside and start down the stairs, two at a time.

"Ms. Morgan," Agent Townsend yells from below. "You're late."

"Sorry," I tell him. I hold up my report. "Almost finished," I say, but he doesn't care about the paperwork.

He nods toward the boy who looks like him. "We have a lead on a rogue asset outside of Kabul. CIA wants the two of you. If you have the time?" Townsend asks, almost condescendingly.

The boy looks at me and smiles. "What do you say, Gallagher Girl. Do you?"

I take the file from Townsend's hand.

"Let's go."

Acknowledgments

The Gallagher Girls would never have been possible without the support and encouragement of everyone at Disney-Hyperion, with special thanks to Catherine Onder, who has seen this series through to the end. Also, Stephanie Lurie, Dina Sherman, Elizabeth Mason, Elke Villa, Holly Nagel, Andrew Sansone, Monica Mayper, Marybeth Tregarthen, Sara Liebling, Marci Senders, Whitney Manger, Julie Moody, and the very talented people who do everything from designing covers to correcting typos. You are all Gallagher Girls and Blackthorne Boys in my book.

I am exceedingly grateful to Kristin Nelson for first inquiring as to whether or not I'd ever consider writing for young adults and for her amazing support in all the days that have followed. I'd also like to thank the people of the Nelson Agency who work so tirelessly on my behalf. Also, Jenny Meyer, Whitney Lee, and Kassie Evashevski.

Perhaps the biggest change in my life between now and eight years ago is that now I have a fantastic group of friends, many of whom were so much help in finishing this final book: Jennifer Lynn Barnes, Holly Black, Sarah Rees Brennan, Rose Brock, Carrie Ryan, Melissa de la Cruz, and, of course, BOB. I'd like to give a special thanks to E. Lockhart for suggesting the title of this novel.

As always, my family is the key to every good thing that has ever happened to me. So Mom, Dad, Amy, Rick, Faith, and Lily, thank you for everything.

And, finally, I thank the librarians, booksellers, parents, and teens who have welcomed the Gallagher Girls into your lives. It has been a pleasure spending my time at the Gallagher Academy with you.